RUSTY AT RAM'S HORN RANCH

Books by Shannon Garst

RUSTY AT RAM'S HORN RANCH

WISH ON AN APPLE

COWBOY BOOTS

SILVER SPURS FOR COWBOY BOOTS

RUSTY

AT RAM'S HORN RANCH

by Shannon Garst

ILLUSTRATED BY RAYMOND CREEKMORE

Abingdon-Cokesbury Press

NEW YORK • NASHVILLE

TO BUNNY

CONTENTS

RUSTY AT RAM'S HORN RANCH

How empty the world seemed! How alone he was!

I

Alone

The boy riding the sorrel horse shivered as he pulled his worn gray jacket tighter about his neck and hunched his shoulders against the gusts of cold wind. His unhappy blue eyes swept the desolate Colorado plains. They stretched for miles to the distant range of mountains, which looked as if they might have been cut from blue cardboard and set up at the edge of the world. The range land was still brown and barren, though here and there a faint greenish tinge to the grass gave hint of spring.

How empty the world seemed! How alone he was!

"Get along, Toby." John jerked the reins, noticing how thin and frightened his voice sounded in this great, silent world.

He had been riding for hour upon hour without seeing

a dwelling. He had not eaten since daybreak, and then only a piece of dry bread. The sun was sinking low. Soon it would be dark. It seemed as if he would have to spend the night on the prairie—hungry, cold, and miserable.

The sorrel jerked on the slackening reins, trying to crop the brown grass at the side of the road. John pulled his head up and reached over to pat the shaggy neck.

"I know you're tired and hungry, Toby," he said gently. "I am, too. More than you are. I let you graze at noon, you know. We've got to keep going until we find a ranch or else we'll have to stay out all night."

He tried hard to keep up his hope that soon they would come to a house. And he made an effort to shove into the back of his mind the idea that his not finding one was somehow a punishment for running away.

No. He was doing right. He knew that he was. Yet he could not help feeling guilty. He was mixed up about the whole thing.

Bitter memories flooded his thoughts. In his twelve years of life there had been few bright spots. The main one was the dim but lovely picture of his golden-haired mother bending over his bed, tucking him in, smiling down at him. Since his mother had died before he was four, he could not be sure whether this was really a memory or something he had imagined.

The other memories, though, were real and terrible. Tod David, his father, was a rough, unschooled man of violent temper. With his even wilder brother, Lon, he caught wild horses in Wyoming and Montana. As soon as John was old

12

enough, he had helped with the roundups and the dangerous work of breaking broomtails. His own sorrel, Toby, he had caught as a colt and broken to ride.

A wild stallion had thrown John's father and pawed him to death. The boy shut his eyes against the memory of that scene.

He had been sent for a while to a boys' home where his bright red hair, his freckles, his stammering had set him apart as one to be teased. And because his tormentors saw how effective their taunts were, he knew no peace. He grew to believe that he was different from others—that it was impossible for anyone to like him. Later he had lived with his uncle, who had worked him hard and used him as someone on whom to vent his violent temper.

Then had come the day when the wild-horse roundup had yielded a splendid golden stallion. John's uncle had licked his lips greedily.

"That big boy will put money in my pocket," he said. "He's worth more than the rest of the lot together."

"He doesn't look like a broomtail to me," John had been unwise enough to say. "Maybe he's a runaway from some ranch."

"Shut your smart-aleck mouth," Lon had roared.

Later the animals were being run through a squeeze chute—a narrow runway with gates front and rear—to be branded. Once inside, the horse was held as though in a vise. To make the job of branding easier, Lon stood astride the rails and dropped a lasso over the head of the horse, choking it until it was too weak to struggle. It was John's

13

job then to slap the branding iron against the neck, where the mane would cover it—the usual place to brand horses.

It took Lon and two helpers to choke down the golden stallion.

"Slap on the iron quick, you dumb kid!" Lon had shrieked.

John had the hot iron raised and ready. But when he saw the X Bar brand already on the sweat-drenched neck, he held back.

"This horse has a brand," he shouted up to his uncle.

"Put my brand over it," Lon ordered. "Be quick about it. I don't want to choke this horse to death."

John deliberately turned and thrust his branding iron back into the fire. He was not going to put his uncle's brand on another man's property.

The next thing he knew he was picking himself up from the ground. His jaw felt as if it had been hit by a giant hammer. Then he heard the stallion scream, smelled burning hair and flesh, and knew that the golden horse now bore a worked-over brand.

John raised a hand to stroke his sore jaw. Then his unhappy memories were wiped out as he topped a rise and saw a sheep wagon to his left.

"We're near a ranch!" he shouted. He straightened up in the saddle. His heels urged Toby to a faster pace. "We'll come to the gate soon. Hurry up!"

Then, finally, there it was! Over the gate was a sign painted in black letters: RAM'S HORN RANCH. And over the sign was a pair of ancient, crumpled ram's horns.

14

Just inside the gate a black-and-white dog sat peering anxiously up the road, as though waiting for someone.

John leaned over, loosened the wire, and swung the gate open. Inside, he dismounted and held out a hand in friendliness to the dog.

"Good old boy," he said. "Nice fellow!"

But the black-and-white dog bared his teeth, snarled, and backed away.

John felt as if he had been slapped by his best friend. He turned and put his hand on the horse's neck.

"Not even a dog likes me," he said in a quiet, choked tone. "I must be pretty bad if even a dog won't like me. You like me, don't you, Toby?"

The horse only nickered with impatience and jerked his head. John climbed quickly into the saddle and urged the pony to a gallop.

They must hurry if they were to reach the ranch buildings before it was completely dark. Ahead John could hear the baaing of sheep and the tinkle of bells. Probably a sheepherder, bedding down his flock. If he did not find the ranch buildings, John thought, he could seek out the wagon. Soon the sheepherder would light his lantern to cook supper. The thought of food made John swallow.

He kept Toby at a gallop, knowing that the horse could rest and graze before very long. He tried hard to push out of his mind the unfriendly actions of the dog at the gate. But the hurt was still there. Would he be unwanted and disliked wherever he went? Surely if he worked hard, tried to do everything right, kept out of people's way, they would give him the food he needed and let him sleep in a shed.

At last he topped a little rise and there, in the bowl-like valley below, lights twinkled. They came from several buildings, standing shadowy against the line of the darker shrubbery which undoubtedly edged a creek.

Toby quickened his pace.

When he came close to the building where the lights were brightest, John could hear voices. He dismounted and dropped the reins.

His mouth grew dry and his heart began to beat fast. The familiar tense feeling took hold of him at the prospect of meeting strangers, but hunger lent him extra courage.

He knocked on the door, timidly at first, then louder.

The door was opened, and a black-haired boy stood in the patch of light.

"Hi!" the boy said. "Come in."

John stepped inside. He blinked at the row of faces lined up on both sides of the long table. His mouth watered at the smell of food.

"Howdy," said a black-haired man at the head of the table. The resemblance was so marked that John was sure he was the father of the boy who had opened the door. Beside the man sat a girl in whom the family resemblance was likewise strong.

John gulped and squirmed in discomfort as everyone stared at him.

"Can I do something for you?" the big man asked.

"Y-yes. I-I—w-want a j-job."

The girl giggled. Her father gave her a meaning look.

16

Everyone stared at him. . . . "I-I w-want a job."

"Careful, Ginger," he warned.

"How old are you?" the man asked.

"F-f-fifteen."

The man raised his black eyebrows in surprise. "You don't say? I wouldn't guess you were a day over twelve."

Crimson flooded John's face. Several of the men snickered.

"Well, we won't bother about that now," the man said kindly. "Melissa, we have another customer for supper. Get him a plate and tools, will you please?"

"M-my horse. Ou-outs-s-side," the boy stammered.

"Of course. Tend your horse first," the man said. "Then wash up at the bench outside the door and come in and eat. Ben, go along and show him where to water and pasture his horse. We'll save some food for you."

"I'm eleven," Ben said when they were outside. "I betcha you were lying when you said you were fifteen. How old are you?"

"Old enough to work," John said curtly. Old enough to mind my own business, he wanted to add, but managed to hold his tongue. "I'd like a job with your dad's outfit," he said. "If I do my work, what does it matter how old I am?"

Ben did not seem a bit offended by the boy's manner. Instead he laughed as he showed John where to water the horse and put the saddle. Then he opened the gate into the pasture.

"I reckon your horse can skip his rubdown tonight," Ben said. "He can roll in the dust and rub the sweat off."

On the way back to the cookhouse Ben went on with his

18

chatter. "You're kind of standoffish, aren't you? But I hope Dad gives you a job anyway."

"How many men work here?"

"Only four now. Besides the four sheepherders who live in wagons. But we start lambing in about a week. After that, we'll have the shearing crew spread all over the place. That's why I think Dad'll give you a job. He needs all the hands he can get and he isn't too choosy about their ages. He says a lively kid can do plenty of work if he's not lazy."

"I'm not lazy," John said as he splashed cold water over his face from the washbasin beside the door.

They stepped inside. The men moved up the bench to make room for them.

"I'm Bruce Leonard," the boss said. "This is Mrs. Leonard." He waved his hand toward the brown-eyed, brown-haired, tired-looking woman who was bustling about the room, waiting on the men. "She's the boss at Ram's Horn. This is Ginger, Ben's twin sister. She tries to boss the place, too. This is our cook, Nellie McAlester, the real boss of the outfit. We all step around when she speaks."

Everyone laughed, and John felt himself relaxing in the friendly atmosphere.

"You'll get acquainted with the men when you go to the bunkhouse." Mr. Leonard waved his hand casually, taking them all in. "You wouldn't remember their names now anyway."

Then abruptly he said, "I don't believe I caught your name."

The boy was caught offguard. Why hadn't he decided beforehand what to call himself?

"D-D-David J-J-Jones." He ducked his head, conscious of hot color flushing his cheeks.

"Say!" Ben cried out. "How come? You stutter now. But you didn't stutter a bit when we were outside."

For once in his life John was willing to have attention called to his stammering. Perhaps Mr. Leonard would not notice how flustered he had been about his name.

"He's embarrassed among so many strangers," Mrs. Leonard said kindly as she placed a glass of milk before John's place. "Don't pester him, Ben. We do take our hats off in the house, though," she went on, looking at the tight-fitting cap which John had failed to remove.

He reached up and in a half-defiant manner yanked off the cap. When his head was bared, several of the men laughed.

Ben shouted, "Ho! You really are a redhead, aren't you? We'd better be careful or you'll set fire to the place."

"And he has freckles to match his hair." The man named Walt grinned with one side of his mouth. "Yours is really the reddest hair I ever did see anywhere. And I've been around. We'll have to call you Rusty."

John's face flamed to match his despised hair. His throat tightened. He couldn't swallow. He was about to push away from the table and flee into the night, but Bruce Leonard's glance held him back.

"They don't mean anything by their teasing," the boss said. "You'll have to learn to take a lot of joshing if you expect a job in the range country. Cattlemen and sheepmen couldn't live without razzing each other. Evidently you're a stranger to our ways."

John's head was still bowed over his plate, but he managed to flash the boss a quick sideways look of gratitude. Slowly he put food into his mouth. Gradually the huge lump which had come into his throat eased away and he could swallow again.

For a while there was an uncomfortable silence. Then the men began to tease each other. The boy realized that they were doing it for his benefit, to show him that they razzed each other just for the fun of it. Little by little the tenseness eased from his body. He relaxed and enjoyed the hunks of boiled beef and potatoes, the cole slaw, stewed tomatoes, rolls, and finally apple pie.

Already he liked it here. Oh, if only Bruce Leonard would let him stay! He would work harder than anyone had ever worked for the boss. The little taste of kindness he had received made him feel that at last he had found the place he had been longing for—a place where he could really belong. Somehow he would make himself important to Mr. and Mrs. Leonard—and to Ginger and Ben, too. Maybe in time he would earn a place of his own in this nice family.

Then he caught his thoughts up short. He was being a fool again, to allow himself such dreams. He was only paving the way for more hurts. He must learn to be hard-boiled—to take what came and not care too much how things turned out. That was the best way. People would make fun of him. They always had. Even people who did not intend to be mean. Besides his freckles, red hair, and stammering, he was a runt—undernourished, undersized, and ridiculously thin. In fact, he thought, there wasn't anything about him that was just right.

After everyone was through eating, the men wandered off to the bunkhouse.

John stood up, uncertain what to do.

"I want to have a talk with you," Mr. Leonard said. "But first, what are we going to call you? David or Rusty?"

The corners of his eyes wrinkled as he stared down at the boy.

John gulped a couple of times and then managed a shy grin. He looked up at the boss and said, "R-R-Rusty, I r-r-reckon."

"I reckon so." The man grinned as he rumpled the fiery hair. "You'd better accept any nickname the men want to give you. After all, a nickname is usually a sign of affection."

Rusty looked startled and then pleased. He hadn't ever thought of it this way.

"Come into my office with me," Mr. Leonard said.

Rusty followed him into a shabby but comfortable room. He noticed the large fireplace, some large, leather-covered chairs, and a sofa over which was thrown an Indian blanket.

Ben and Ginger peered around the doorway, their dark eyes sparkling with mischief and curiosity.

"This is a private business talk," their father said, shutting the door. "You kids help your mother and Nellie with the dishes."

"Sit down." Bruce Leonard motioned to one of the great leather chairs. Rusty perched uneasily on the edge.

"Now out with it," Mr. Leonard said. "Let's not beat about the bush. Who are you?"

Rusty's mouth became a tight line. "I-I-I-" he began.

"Take it slowly. Whistle," the boss said in an unconcerned tone.

"I—m-my name is D-David J-J . . ."

"Yes, I know." A smile tugged at the man's lips. "David Jones. A nice anonymous name. And you're fifteen. But I don't believe you. You're really about twelve, aren't you?"

Rusty nodded.

"And your real name?"

Again the lips tightened. John lowered his eyes to study his fingernails.

"I suppose you ran away from home?"

The lips came together tighter, but the boy said not a word.

"All right then." Mr. Leonard tilted back in his chair. "When you get ready, you tell me the whole story. Meantime we'll call you Rusty Jones. You can be roustabout— chore boy—around here for a few days, until you get homesick."

"I won't get h-homesick. Ever!" the boy said with a violence that made the man whistle.

"Whew! You must have had quite a row with your dad —or someone. But you'll get over it."

Rusty shook his head, but would say no more.

"Talkative young rascal, aren't you?" the boss said.

23

"Well, here in the range country we don't ask many questions about a man's past. Who he was or what he did a month ago doesn't matter to us. We're interested in what he is now. That's all that matters."

The boy relaxed slightly under the man's keen dark eyes.

"But," Mr. Leonard went on cautiously, "if you've done something I ought to know about—better get it off your chest. It may make it easier."

Rusty shook his head and looked up appealingly.

"All right then. But I'm ready to listen any time you want to talk. And of course, since you're under age, I'll have to send word to town to the sheriff that I have a kid of your description here. Just in case anyone is looking for you."

"N-no one w-will look for me," Rusty said.

There was such a load of bitterness in the young voice that Bruce Leonard whistled again in surprise.

"I've a notion that you've had rather a rough time," he said. "But if you're a willing worker, you'll have a job here for the summer—or until someone comes and gets you."

Rusty said nothing more, but he gave the man a grateful look.

Mr. Leonard opened the door.

"Ben," he called. "Show Rusty the way to the bunkhouse."

II

Boy of Mystery

Rusty followed Ben into the bunkhouse. It was warm and cozy inside. The round heating stove at one end of the room took away the early spring chill, and the Mazda lamp hanging from the ceiling made a pleasant pool of light.

"Here's Rusty, fellows," Ben said importantly. "Rusty, that's Mont Brill, our foreman."

He pointed to a man sitting on one of the bunks, sewing a button on a blue shirt. He was tall, lean, and forceful looking. Rusty liked his appearance, especially when he looked up and smiled with a friendly expression.

"Hi, Rusty," he said casually. "Glad to have you with us. Come in."

Rusty stepped inside.

" 'Night," Ben said.

With a bang of the door he was gone, leaving Rusty alone to face the four pairs of eyes staring at him.

"Ah, Torch-head in person," one of the men remarked. The boy noticed the way one side of his mouth turned down and the other side turned up.

"Get the water bucket. The place is on fire!" another man cried in mock alarm.

Rusty stood with his back to the door. "H-h-howdy, f-f-fellows." He did his best to sound friendly.

"Come right on in, Rusty," Mont said. "I reckon this bunk right over mine is reserved just for you. Sit down any place and make yourself at home."

Rusty perched gingerly on the edge of the bunk on which Mont was sitting. "That's Walt Norton sewing a patch on his levis," the foreman said.

This was the sandy-haired man who wore a perpetual grin with one side of his mouth while the other side turned down.

"That's Juan Lopez." The foreman pointed to the kindly-looking Mexican strumming a guitar.

"I pleez to meet," Juan said in a soft voice.

"And that handsome guy reading the Western magazine is Willie Smith."

"Howdy, Rusty," Willie said.

Rusty had been struck by this man's appearance at the table. Surely he must be a thug—or a very rough character. His nose was flattened and twisted to one side and his upper lip had a cruel scar which pulled it up in what appeared to be a snarl. Yet he turned and there was a genuine-ly friendly look in his blue eyes.

"You mustn't mind when we josh you," Willie said. "We do it for amusement and to keep our minds off of how gosh-awful looking we are. You look scared to death. Relax. You're among friends, Rusty."

Sudden warmth flooded the boy's heart. Willie was swell. He must hate his battered face, just as he, John, hated his hair and his small size. And now he liked the name Rusty. It had a manly ring to it—a nickname without the hateful undertones of Red, Carrottop, Firetop, and other of the detested names people had called him. It showed, as Bruce Leonard had pointed out, that those who used it liked him a bit.

Their greetings over, the men went on with whatever they had been doing. Rusty curled up on the bunk and listened to the talk. It was mostly about sheep. All of these men, it was plain, had worked with sheep for years. They knew all the peculiarities of flocks and individual sheep, sheepherders, and dogs.

When the talk came around to herders and their dogs, Rusty straightened up with interest.

"Tom Comfort says that his dog Jack can count," Willie remarked, "and sometimes it seems almost as if he can. He sure knows when any sheep are missing and goes out aft-er 'em."

"Jack's one of the best sheep dogs I ever saw," Walt agreed. "Pancho has a good sheep dog, too. The only trouble is that he can't understand English—only Spanish."

27

"That was a fine dog the boss had a few years back," Mont put in. "The winter he lost a herder in a blizzard. The dog stuck right with the herd. He couldn't stop them from drifting, but he kept them together the best he could. And he was there with what was left of them when the boss found them three days later."

"It's training that makes a good sheep dog," Walt said.

"Shucks," Willie contradicted him. "If you happen onto a dog that comes from a line of good sheep dogs, you hardly have to train him. He knows by instinct what to do."

"It seems that way sometimes," Mont agreed. "If a dog isn't willing to work, it's usually a waste of time to try to make him. Though I've seen good trainers make workers out of dogs that others had cast off."

"W-what about that d-dog b-by the g-gate?" Rusty inquired.

He was shy at intruding himself into the men's talk, but bursting with curiosity about the dog he had seen.

"He looks like a fine Border collie," Mont said. "They're a breed brought originally from Scotland, and the best for working with sheep. But it's my guess that dog's been ruined by mistreatment. He won't have anything to do with any of us, though Ben feeds him every day."

The men all agreed that once a sensitive dog's confidence in man had been shaken or his proud spirit broken, he could never be cured.

Rusty wished that the talk about dogs would go on and on. But now the men were yawning and stretching and removing their boots, making ready to go to bed.

By the time breakfast was over the next morning, much of Rusty's feeling of strangeness had eased away. He did not say anything unless it was absolutely necessary, because of the embarrassment his stuttering caused him. And he knew that the harder he tried to control it, the more he stammered. Yet sometimes, when he was especially interested in what he was talking about, he was not bothered at all.

When breakfast was over, Mr. Leonard told Rusty that he could help Ben with the chores and make himself useful wherever he could.

The man stared down at Rusty, studying him. Then he said, "Maybe I'd better see how good a worker you are before I make any agreement about pay. I'll be fair, I promise you that. And I expect you to be the same."

Rusty looked up at the boss with a shy smile. He would have been willing to work without pay. A warm place to sleep, nourishing food, and kind treatment were more than he had ever had.

As they were getting up from the table, Rusty saw Ben put the table scraps onto a tin pan, which he carried outside. Curious, Rusty followed. Ben put the pan down by a tree stump and whistled. Soon the black-and-white dog crept from a clump of bushes. He looked around timidly, then made a dash for the food and downed it in a gulp or two.

"Gee whillikers!" Rusty gasped. "He sure acts hungry. As if he hadn't been fed for a week. Come here, fellow."

But the dog was off into the bushes like a black-and-white streak.

"He comes here for food every day," Ben explained. "But he won't make friends with anyone. He's wild as a coyote. He looks like a Border collie. They're the best sheep dogs alive. But something happened to ruin him."

"What do you suppose it was?" asked Rusty.

"He was beaten or treated mean," Ben guessed. "Or maybe he was a one-man dog who got lost from his master. For weeks he's been waiting by our gate for someone to come back. At first he nearly starved. Dad talked about shooting him for fear hunger would make a sheep killer out of him. But Ginger and I tried taking food out to him every day. Each day we put it a bit nearer the house. After a while he'd come into the yard. But still he won't make friends with any of us."

"I saw him when I came in the gate," Rusty said. "He wouldn't make friends with me either. He snarled at me and I thought he didn't like me." Rusty was pleased that the dog's unfriendliness was not a personal matter.

One of Rusty's chores was to pump water and carry bucketfuls to the kitchen. Another was to chop wood and carry armloads of it to the kitchen to feed the huge range on which the meals were cooked.

Mrs. McAlester, the cook, and Mrs. Leonard bustled about making bread and pies. Rusty learned that their day commenced at five o'clock in the morning and ended late at night, after the supper dishes were done. During all that time they worked as hard and fast as they could, except for a brief rest in the afternoon. Mrs. Leonard looked too frail for such hard work, but Nellie McAlester seemed sturdy

enough, and apparently enjoyed her own cooking.

Mrs. Leonard looked up from her work and smiled at the two boys as they dumped their armloads of wood into the box by the stove.

"I've always wanted a redheaded, freckle-faced boy," she said to Rusty. "Somehow they've always seemed sort of extra special to me."

Rusty smiled shyly. Funny! There had been times when those had been fighting words, but it sounded nice to have

Mrs. Leonard call him redheaded and freckled. Maybe she really meant it—that she liked the very things which had made him laughed at and made fun of. His heart warmed. She was the nicest woman he had ever known!

Ginger looked up from her potato-peeling resentfully. "As soon as I get through peeling these spuds," she said sulkily, "I'll be with you." She eyed her mother as she spoke.

"After you fill and clean the lamps and set the table," her mother said mildly.

"Ginger hates kitchen work," Ben explained when they were outside. "She likes to work outdoors. She should've been a boy."

Rusty's heart fell a bit. He was beginning to enjoy Ben's company. Having a girl around would spoil it. Girls were no fun.

"It's kind of quiet around here now," Ben explained. "But it won't be long until things begin to boom. Lambing will start next week. Then everyone will be running his legs off and not getting much sleep."

"Sounds exciting," Rusty said.

"You said a mouthful, brother." Ben nodded his head. "I hope you stay." He gave Rusty a sideways look.

"Why?" Rusty's blue eyes widened. "Is-is your father thinking of firing me?"

Ben shrugged. "No. I don't think so. Only—"again that sly, sideways look—"naturally he wonders who you are. And why you're so mysterious about everything. He thinks you ran away from home, or got in some sort of trouble and will be picked up or something. Say! Were you in a reform school?"

Rusty stopped in his tracks. His face reddened. He clenched his fists and his jaw jutted out fiercely. "W-w-wouldn't you like to know?" he growled. "W-w-wouldn't y-you j-just like to know?"

Ben's dark eyes widened, too. "Yeh. Sure I'd like to know," he said reasonably. "You make me curious. But you don't have to tell. Dad said you'd tell about yourself when you got ready. Don't get so huffy."

The rage which had flared up in Rusty died down. Why had he almost lost his temper again, just because Ben had asked him a perfectly natural question? Ben was really a swell guy—open and above board about everything.

"Ask me no questions and I'll t-tell you no lies," he said, trying to smile.

"O.K.," Ben said good-naturedly. "Go ahead and be a mystery guy if you want to. You remind me of Lone Wolf —that's what we call the dog who won't make friends."

"Only I don't have any m-man I'm waiting for," Rusty said with bitterness.

"Well, anyway," Ben said brightly, "I hope you stay. It'll be fun to have another kid around."

Rusty grinned his appreciation.

"Let's go over to the corral," Ben suggested. "Randy Burke was coming over today to take the kinks out of the horses that have been on the range all winter. We'll need to use them during lambing. They're pretty full of snorts when they've been running wild."

Ben lengthened his stride, and Rusty hurried along beside him. Some riders were driving a herd of horses down a hillside into the bowl in which the ranch buildings nestled. It was a pretty sight to see them running, raising a veil of dust, their manes and tails flying.

Shouting and waving their hats, the men hazed the horses into a corral. One man swung the gate shut.

A slim young man, wearing a big hat, sat on the top of the corral fence. His high-heeled boots were hooked over one of the poles. His hat was pushed back from a dark, handsome face with a devil-may-care expression. He wore tight-fitting levis, a red plaid shirt and a red bandanna neckerchief, and a wide carved leather belt with a huge silver buckle.

Rusty's eyes rested on Randy's boots with their red tops gay with embroidered butterflies. They were the fanciest things Rusty had ever seen. His heart missed a beat. Here was an honest-to-goodness cowboy. In person!

Ben clambered to the top rail and perched there beside Randy. Rusty lost no time in climbing up beside him.

"Howdy, fellow railbirds," the cowboy drawled. His dark eyes twinkled. "I reckon you want to learn to be cowboys."

"We just came to watch the show," Ben said. Rusty noticed a note of stiffness in his voice.

Randy looked across at Rusty. "Hi there, Carrottop," he grinned. "I can see that you have the makin's of a real cowboy. I never yet saw a redhead who couldn't be a good cowboy if he made up his mind to it."

The horse put on a bucking exhibition

Rusty, instead of resenting the reference to his red hair, was pleased with it, coming from the cowboy. But Ben put in, "Aw, cut out that grand cowboy stuff! We're sheepmen in this spread. And proud of it!"

Randy shrugged. "There's no accounting for tastes," he remarked. "But I notice that when you want the rough edges taken off your horses, you call on a regular he-man to do the job."

He slid from the fence, putting an end to the conversation. His rope snaked out and around the neck of a brown horse which had just been driven into the corral. The other end of the rope was quickly wound around the snubbing post in the center, a saddle was slapped on the quivering back, and Randy was in the saddle while the rope was being loosened.

The horse put on a bucking exhibition which had Rusty's heart in his throat. But it did not last long. In a few moments Randy was on the back of another bucker. Ginger clambered onto the fence as the second horse was being ridden.

"H-he's a crackajack!" Rusty exclaimed.

"Huh!" Ben snorted. "Those horses aren't wild. They're just kind of springy from not being worked for so long. Randy sure likes to show off. He thinks being a rodeo rider is the most wonderful thing in the world."

"It must be pretty exciting," Rusty said.

"Oh, sure," Ben said. "But it makes me mad the way cowboys look down on sheepmen. We ran cattle for a while. And running sheep has the cattle business backed off the map when it comes to excitement, even if Randy doesn't think so."

Ginger had joined them. "It's because they're always making movies of cowboys," she explained. "They dress the cowboys up fancy and have them always singing, and stuff like that. Maybe sheepherders aren't so romantic— but they're pretty wonderful people."

She looked at Randy defiantly. "No cowboy would go through what some of our herders have to save their sheep," she added.

Rusty looked at Ginger in surprise. Maybe for a girl she had pretty good sense. But when he turned his gaze back to the cowboy seated on the bucking horse, waving his hat, spurring the horse to make it buck harder, he was sure that he had never seen so dashing and romantic a figure. Excitement ran through his veins. This was living! He knew quite a bit about riding horses and he recognized that Randy was good.

"Dad hasn't much use for Randy," Ben explained. "Thinks he's kind of worthless. He's a sort of grub-line runner during the winter. That is, he rides from one ranch to another, mooching grub and board. Then all summer he follows the rodeos. And he's good enough so that he makes a living at it."

"He *is* good," Rusty said. "Oh boy, he really is good!"

"Yeh," Ben admitted. "He can ride all right. But it's all he does. And he *is* a drifter. I guess I'd like him, though, if he wasn't always running us sheepmen down. We're proud of running a sheep outfit."

That evening Rusty saddled Toby to ride to the mailbox to get the mail.

"Get up, Toby!" His heels pounded the pony's sides. Rusty wished Toby would kick up his heels a bit. Ginger was watching from the kitchen window and he wanted her to see that he could ride a lively horse.

But Toby only lay back his ears, jerked at the reins, and refused to buck.

III

High Speed at Ram's Horn

Day by day life at the Ram's Horn Ranch grew busier as lambing season approached. Gradually Rusty settled into the routine. He noticed that the men joshed each other a great deal, and that if anyone showed he was bothered by the teasing, he got an even larger dose. Most of the men were good-natured about it. Rusty made up his mind that he would be good-natured too. And he noticed that when he was, the men teased him less.

Mr. and Mrs. Leonard, he decided, were the nicest people he had ever known. They worked very hard. Often Mrs. Leonard appeared nearly ready to drop from exhaustion. Yet the Leonards were never irritable or ill-tempered. Always they seemed to have time to be kind and considerate. Rusty had never known such people before.

The first evening, when he was milking, Rusty knocked over a full bucket of milk. He had never handled cows and was awkward in milking. Mr. Leonard was nearby when it happened. Passing him, Rusty ducked. Bruce Leonard caught him by the shoulder.

"You've done that several times," he said, his eyes searching Rusty's face.

"I-I d-didn't m-mean to k-knock the m-milk over," Rusty said, trembling. "I-it's the first time."

"I didn't mean that. I mean that you often dodge as though you expected me to strike you."

"I-I sure thought y-you w-w-would when I knocked over the m-m-milk," Rusty said.

"No. I wouldn't hit you for making mistakes. Do your best, and you needn't be afraid of me."

"G-gee! I'm s-s-sorry I did it."

"Of course you're sorry. I am, too. But I don't think it will happen again."

Rusty's heart filled with warm gratitude. He made a point, however, of trading chores with Ben so that he would not have to milk.

The lone wolf dog still came every day for food, then ran off into the bushes to hurry down the road and wait by the gate for the master who never came. Rusty asked Ben to let him take the pan of food to the pitiful creature.

"Sure," Ben agreed. "I've forgotten him a couple of times. We have so many dogs around."

The animal was often in Rusty's thoughts. The dog was so much like himself—homeless and friendless, though now being kindly treated. If only he could make the dog lose his fear and accept kindness and friendliness! Rusty tried very hard to make friends with the dog, but he seemed to make no headway at all.

One evening, while he was holding out the pan of food, Mont came from the cookshack. Lone Wolf peered from between the bushes. He wore a famished look on his face, but he would not come near until the person who was feeding him was far out of reach.

"He'll never make up to you," Mont said seriously. "He's a sure-enough one-man dog. Someone's mistreated him and he's lost faith in everyone but his master."

Rusty looked interested.

"Anyone who mistreats a dog ought to be shot," Mont went on. "They're such fine, loyal creatures if folks are halfway decent to them. Maybe he was a good sheep dog— or could have been trained to be one."

"Th-that's what I th-thought," Rusty said seriously. "I w-want to make fr-friends with him. Then I can train him to help Mr. L-Leonard w-with the sheep."

A smile tugged at the corners of Mont's mouth. "It's a good enough idea," he said. "But I'm afraid you're wasting your time. Once a dog or a horse is ruined, you can never make it worth its salt again."

He gave Rusty a long, level look. "I reckon it's only a human being who has guts enough to rise above a broken spirit. I think a person can make himself just about the sort of man he makes up his mind to be."

Rusty stared up into Mont's eyes. The foreman seemed

to be putting considerable weight into what he was saying —as if he meant it to sink deep into the listener's mind to take root there.

But probably he was imagining things, Rusty thought, as Mont strode away toward the barn.

Rusty eased himself to the ground and held out the pan. "Come on, fellow. Oh, please come on and let's be friends," he begged. "No one will hurt you."

He squatted there, pleading, a world of kindness in his voice. His muscles ached, but he did not want to move for fear of frightening the dog away.

After what seemed an endless time, the dog began to crawl closer. Several times he turned and ran. Then he would begin to crawl along on his belly again, each time coming a little closer.

Rusty gritted his teeth to keep from moving his tortured leg muscles. At last the dog was close. He stretched forth his neck, seized a hunk of meat, and gulped it while Rusty still held the pan. Then quickly he gulped everything on the plate. Rusty expected him to turn tail and run. Instead, to his amazement, the dog looked into his eyes with a world of yearning. Then he put his head on Rusty's knee. Gradually, lightly, Rusty placed his hand on the dog's head. Then slowly he moved his hand to rub the black ear.

A low whimper came from the dog's throat.

"It's all right," Rusty told him. "We're two of a kind. And now we're friends. We'll be friends forever."

Now it seemed that the dog could not get enough petting. He shoved closer and closer. He whined and licked Rusty's hand with gratitude.

Mr. and Mrs. Leonard came to the door. The stir they made startled the dog and he ran into the bushes.

"Well I never!" Mrs. Leonard exclaimed.

"I never saw anything like it," her husband echoed. "I didn't suppose anyone could ever make friends with that poor creature."

"But now he's gone!" Rusty wailed.

"He'll come back," Bruce Leonard said. "He's still afraid of us, but you've won his confidence. He'll not be afraid of you again. He's your dog."

Rusty stood up. He stretched his cramped leg muscles, although unaware now of their aching. "Can I-I have him?" he cried breathlessly. "F-for my own?"

"He's yours," Bruce Leonard repeated. "He's adopted you. I shouldn't wonder if you'd have a hard time to get rid of him if you wanted to. And I imagine he won't have much to do with any of the rest of us."

A great lump came into Rusty's throat and he couldn't talk. Now he had a real friend. A dog of his very own. A dog that would be his alone.

Once he had conquered a wild colt—Toby. He had made himself its master. And for a while he had felt himself a king. Toby meant much to him. And having won the friendship of this frightened dog made his heart glow with warmth.

"I-I'll c-call him Pal," he said softly when he was able to speak again.

"That's a good name," Mrs. Leonard said. "I'm sure that he'll be a fine pal for you."

Now Rusty set about in earnest to win the confidence of the dog. He often whispered to him when he had his arm about his neck. He told Pal: "Mont Brill says that an animal that has been ruined by abuse never amounts to anything. We've got to prove that he's wrong about that. Even if it's true about other dogs—you're different, you are."

Mont's words that night had made a strong impression on Rusty's mind. He often repeated them to himself: "Only a human being has guts enough to rise above a broken spirit. . . . A person can make himself the sort of man he wants to be."

Rusty resolved to prove the truth of that statement. He would rise above his once broken spirit. He would become a man of importance. And he would help Pal rise above his broken spirit and become one of the beloved work dogs of the Ram's Horn Ranch.

Pal became Rusty's devoted friend, following at his heels. The dog's adoration did something to Rusty's spirit. He had never been important to anyone or anything before. Many times he had ached with longing to be loved by and necessary to one living thing. Now that wish was granted. Pal's devotion warmed his heart until much of the bitterness and hardness melted away.

From everyone else, the dog cringed. At first Rusty was rather pleased that Pal would have nothing to do with the others. Then he realized that, in order to be a good work dog, Pal would have to hold up his head and take orders from anyone in authority in handling sheep. So he took pains to get him used to others. First he tried with Ben and Ginger, who had fed the dog before Rusty became his master. At last Pal would let them come close and put gentle hands on his head. Then Rusty led him to make friends with the other men, one by one. It was a slow process, requiring much patience. And as the dog's confidence in mankind was being restored, Rusty gained confidence in himself.

One noon Mr. Leonard told Ben, Ginger, and Rusty to go out on horseback to help drive a flock of sheep closer to the lambing sheds. All of the sheep about to lamb were being driven slowly toward headquarters. Small tents were being taken to places where they were likely to be needed, and small corrals of brush were being built here and there about the lambing grounds.

When Rusty went to the corral to get Toby, Randy was there, preparing to take some more kinks out of the horses brought in from the range.

Randy had become Rusty's hero. Rusty never tired of watching him. Rusty decided that someday he would be a rodeo rider. As soon as he had time he would practice riding broncs until he became as good at it as Randy was. The cowboy had a wonderful saddle, heavily trimmed with silver, and a bridle and silver spurs. He often mentioned other trophies he had won in rodeos, as well as money prizes.

Rusty's eyes sparkled as he listened to Randy's tales of how the crowds cheered when he rode the wildest of broncs; how people turned to stare at him when he strode down the street; and how his picture was in hundreds of newspapers. What an exciting, glamorous life it must be!

When Rusty threw his shabby saddle on Toby's back and climbed aboard, Randy threw back his head and laughed. "Don't tell me that moth-eaten old hunk of crowbait is yours," he said. "I've wondered why they kept such an old broomtail on the ranch. I supposed they were saving him to grind up for dog mcat."

The dangerous red flamed into Rusty's face. "Why you—you—you gr-grub-line r-r-rider. M-m-my horse h-has s-speed and st-st-amina a-a-and . . ."

The excitement drove him into such a spell of stuttering that he was unable to talk.

Instantly Randy's face sobered. "Gee, kid, I'm sorry," he said. "I ought to know how a fella feels about a horse he owns. I didn't realize it was your horse. I thought it was one on the ranch that they were letting you ride."

The anger died from Rusty's heart. Why did he have to flare up so easily? Randy was swell!

"Sh-sh-ure enough, Toby's m-my own h-horse." He smiled. "H-he's all mine. And when you c-call him a br-broomtail you tell the truth. I-I h-helped to catch him over in Wyoming. Th-then m-my uncle l-let me break h-him myself."

"You don't say!" the cowboy exclaimed admiringly. "You're some kid to catch and break your own horse. And, believe me, those Wyoming broomtails do have plenty of stamina and spirit and speed. They make the

47

wildest buckers I run into at the rodeos. I have plenty of
respect for those boys. One or two of them have come
near to making me bite the dust."

Feeling much better, and with Randy once more his
hero, Rusty galloped to catch up with Ben and Ginger.

"Let's race," Ginger suggested.

"No. Better not," Ben threw a nod toward Rusty's
horse.

Rusty was quick to catch its meaning. He grinned.

"Oh, y-you don't need to be afraid. Toby here can keep up with you," he shouted. "He may not be much for looks, b-but he's got good stuff."

"All right. Let's go!" Ginger shouted.

She pounded her pony's ribs with her heels, and in a moment the three of them were racing their ponies across the prairie.

For a time Ginger was ahead. Rusty's eyes widened at the way Ginger could ride. Say, she was as good as a boy! Before long Ben's horse nosed ahead of Toby, but Ginger kept in the lead. Ben looked over his shoulder, grinning.

Then slowly Toby commenced to gain. Rusty chuckled. He knew just what would happen. Ben and Ginger were riding good range stock—quarter horses, so named because they could spurt ahead with considerable speed for a quarter of a mile. But Rusty knew they could not keep up that pace much longer. His horse had many times had to depend for its life on its ability to maintain a fast pace for long distances. The prairies on which it had to fight for existence had developed in it a marvelous stamina. Now that stamina began to tell. Before long Toby, the rough-haired pony, was out ahead. Now it was Rusty who was throwing a grin of triumph over his shoulder.

"Say!" Ben shouted when Rusty reined in his pony and the race was over. "That little horse of yours has something."

"Yeh. H-he's a l-long ways from being crowbait," Rusty said. "In fact, h-he's quite a horse."

"He certainly is," Ginger nodded emphatically.

"I never knew a g-girl who could ride l-like you," Rusty said. "You're almost as g-good as a boy."

"That's not too good," Ginger tossed her head. Evidently she was not flattered by what Rusty had intended as a compliment.

IV

Big Brother to a Lamb

After the race, the three riders slowed their horses and allowed them to take their own gait for a time.

"Spring is here. The grass is green." Ginger made a little song of the words.

"The grass has just popped out since I've been here," Rusty remarked.

"Those few rains we've had at night and the hot sun in the daytime bring the grass out in a hurry," Ben said. "I sure hope that we have good weather for lambing and for shearing."

He explained to Rusty: "It all depends on the weather whether Dad has money in the bank or not. Sometimes it's warm like this right up to lambing time. Then it will snow or turn foul in some way and mess up things."

Rusty heard a soft tinkle of bells and the baaing of sheep. He saw a sheep wagon perched on top of a slight rise. When they topped the rise, there in the shallow valley and on the surrounding hilltops he saw groups of sheep. But they were not grazing peacefully, as Rusty supposed they always did. They were running from one patch of green grass to another.

"They always do that when the grass first turns green," Ben explained. "They're so crazy for the stuff that they act like a bunch of lunatics."

"J-jumping grasshoppers!" Rusty exclaimed. "How many thousand are there?"

"About twelve hundred," Ben said. "There are four flocks about that big on the ranch."

Rusty whistled at the thought of so many sheep.

"There's Tom Comfort," Ginger said, and set her horse to a gallop. The other two followed her example.

Rusty heard a dog barking. In a moment a shaggy black-and-white dog appeared from behind a clump of bushes. He was driving several sheep before him. Behind him came the herder, carrying something in his arms.

As they rode toward the man, Ben said to Rusty, "I don't know how old Tom Comfort is—but he looks older than Santa Claus. He's been herding sheep for Dad since long before I was born. He's a nice old fellow."

As they came alongside the white-haired old man, Rusty saw that he held a small, trembling lamb.

"Gee whillikers!" Ben exclaimed. "Have the ewes started to drop their lambs already?"

"It's started," the old herder answered. "This little fellow's mother got bogged down in the marsh back of the willows." His arms cradled the lamb tenderly. "She's back there, about done for. I wrapped her in my jacket. I'm glad you kids happened along. Ben and Ginger, you

53

know what to do. Build a fire in my cookstove in the wagon and get this youngster warm and dry and she may pull through. I'll go back and see if I can save her mamma. You other boy there, ride over to the wagon with Ben and get a blanket from my bed. Then follow me."

"His name's Rusty," Ben said, leaning over to take the tiny lamb from the old man's arms. "He's working for Dad."

"I-I'll hurry w-with the blanket," Rusty said, glad that he was asked to help out.

"Are lambs always reddish like that?" he asked as he rode with Ben and Ginger toward the sheep wagon.

"They are when they're new," Ben replied. "But they soon turn white. Their mammas lick 'em clean."

"I hope the poor little fellow lives." Ginger's voice was husky with pity. "Let me carry him, Ben."

"Nope," Ben said importantly. "You know they shouldn't be handed around. They shouldn't be handled any more than necessary."

Outside the wagon the three dismounted, letting the reins trail while they hurried inside. Ben continued to hold the lamb while Rusty quickly built a fire in the small cookstove. Then Ben picked up a dish towel, wrapped the trembling creature in it, and thrust the bundle into the oven, leaving the door open.

"You aren't going to cook it, are you?" Rusty asked in amazement.

"You'll be surprised how much heat these little fel-

54

lows can soak up," Ben said. "Don't worry. I won't let him get too hot. I've done this before."

Rusty took the blanket which Ginger thrust at him. "You'd better hurry with this," she said.

Rusty galloped to the spot where he had seen the old sheepherder go into a clump of bushes. He found Tom beside a marshy piece of ground, rubbing a ewe with his blue denim jacket.

"Fine! Fine!" Tom Comfort said when Rusty handed him the blanket. "Give me a hand here, will you?"

Rusty knelt beside the man as he bundled the ewe up in the blanket.

"Is—is she dead?" Rusty's eyes were wide.

"Not quite." Tom shook his head. "We may save her. She's pretty weak though. I wouldn't have missed her at all if Jack, my dog, hadn't found her. That Jack is smarter than most people. He can smell out lost sheep better than any dog I ever had. Besides that, he can count."

"Count?" There was a big question mark after the word as Rusty spoke it. He wondered if Tom Comfort was trying to josh him.

"He always knows when any sheep are missing. He couldn't do that unless he was able to count." The herder spoke in such a serious manner that Rusty knew he believed what he was saying. "I'm glad you've got your horse," Tom said. "These old ladies are plenty heavy to lug around. Especially when their fleece is wet."

"You aren't going to stick her in the oven, are you?" Rusty asked.

"I would if I had an oven big enough," the herder said. "But I guess we'll have to let the sun warm her up. Help me heft her onto your horse, will you?"

Rusty helped Tom lift the passive ewe in front of the saddle. Toby looked around with amazed eyes at what was going on, but remained quiet under Rusty's soothing commands.

"You get in the saddle. I'll walk," Rusty said.

The two of them went out into the warm sunlight. Tom Comfort rode to where the sun was warmest, on the side of a hill. He climbed from the saddle, and he and Rusty lifted the ewe to the ground. Then they took turns rubbing her wool with the blanket. When she was partly dried, Tom shoved her onto her feet. Taking hold of her head, he bade Rusty get behind and push. In this way they forced her to walk around.

"This'll help warm her up," Tom said. "She'll be all right if she will help herself a bit."

The pulling and shoving went on for some time. But whenever Tom and Rusty stopped shoving, the ewe sank to the ground with a grunt.

"Maybe I could tie a rope around her neck and let Toby pull her," Rusty suggested.

"Sounds like a good idea—if it works," the herder said. "This old girl is going to have us both worn out."

Rusty climbed into the saddle and let out the lariat he always carried tied to his saddle horn. Tom tied the noose around the ewe's neck and held her on her feet while Rusty eased the horse forward. The ewe held back, but when the pull upon her neck became uncomfortable, she walked to ease the strain.

"It works!" Tom cried. "You're a smart young'un."

Rusty grinned with pleasure.

The warm sun heating her from without and the exercise warming her blood restored the ewe's strength. At Tom's signal Rusty reined his horse to a standstill. The ewe began to crop grass.

"She'll make it," Tom shouted. "That's one of Bruce Leonard's sheep saved."

Rusty could see that the herder was more delighted at having saved this bit of his employer's property than he would have been at saving something of his own. This was a sample of the sheepherder's loyalty which he had heard mentioned so often since he had been at the Ram's Horn.

"You might ride over to the wagon," Tom suggested, "and see how the lamb is. If it's warm and wiggling, it's time it had some nourishment—if we can persuade this old gal to claim her baby."

This surprised Rusty. He had always taken it for granted that ewes were good mothers. But he rode quickly to the wagon, not waiting to ask the questions that were in his mind.

Ben was sitting before the door. Ginger was inside, gazing down at the small creature which was half in, half on, the open door of the oven. Its head was partly up and faint baas came from its mouth.

"Tom Comfort wants me to take the lamb to its

mother," Rusty said with an air of importance.

"Bet she won't claim it," Ben said.

"I kinda hope she doesn't," Ginger said. "Then I'll have a bum lamb to raise."

"As if we wouldn't have enough of those pesky things!" Ben snorted.

Ben held the lamb up for Rusty to take. Ginger and Ben climbed onto their horses to ride over with him and see the mothering-up—if it took place.

Tom took the lamb and placed it so it could nurse. Instinct worked well. Baaing with desperation and pleading, the lamb nuzzled underneath the ewe. But the ewe turned around, baaed resentfully, and butted the impertinent creature.

"She says she never saw the lamb before," Ben snorted. "You can't fool us, old girl."

He dismounted and stood in front of the ewe. Then he took firm hold of her head while Tom Comfort struggled to help the lamb.

But their efforts were in vain. The ewe was evidently a giddy creature who had no natural instinct for motherhood. In fact she glared with positive hatred at the knobby-kneed creature which was trying so hard to attach itself to her.

"You kids take lamby back to the wagon and give it canned milk from a bottle. It'll have to have nourishment pretty quick. Then you'd better take it to the house."

Ginger reached out for the little fellow. "It's mine!"

she cried, snuggling it in her arms. "My first bum lamb of the season."

Ben did not protest. "Just as if the darned things wouldn't be underfoot all over the place before lambing season is over," he snorted in contempt. "You're welcome to this one."

They rode back to the wagon. Ben poured milk from an opened can into a pan and diluted and warmed it. He put the milk into a pop bottle, several of which stood on a shelf over the stove. Over the opening he put a rubber nipple.

Ginger was sitting on one of the benches running along the side of the wagon. She took the bottle and, holding the lamb as if it were a baby, thrust the nipple into its mouth. At first the little creature struggled, but when some of the warm fluid got onto its tongue, it began sucking, its tail jerking with happiness.

"G-gosh!" Rusty exclaimed. "If you have a lot of bum lambs, I should think it would take an awful lot of time to raise 'em."

"It does." Ben nodded his head. "But at the ranch we have a big pan with rubber teats sticking from it. After the lambs get started, they can feed themselves. Of course, when they're as little and weak as this fellow, they have to be fed by hand for a couple of days."

Tom Comfort came to the wagon as the lamb finished the bottle.

"You'd better tell your dad," he said to Ben, "that I'll need some help if he can spare any. Several ewes will drop their lambs tonight. This is a good place to stop over. Good grass and water, and fairly sheltered if the weather holds good."

"The lambing crew hasn't come yet," Ben told Tom with a worried frown. "Dad's afraid someone else has gone to town and hired away from him the men he was promised. He may have to go to town himself, but he just can't spare the time. It's sure tough getting help these days."

"I can stay here and h-help Tom," Rusty said timidly. Ben looked at him and frowned. Then he turned to Tom. "What do you say?" he inquired doubtfully. "Rusty doesn't know a sheep from a woolly dog, but he's awfully willing. Dad says he hasn't got a lazy bone in him."

"He'll do," Tom said. "He's got good sense. And if he'll do what I tell him to, we'll get along all right. Things won't be rushing for a few days. And by that time he'll have learned plenty."

"I'll tell Dad then," Ben said. "I'm sure it'll be all right with him. I'll have him send a truck out tomorrow with supplies. What do you need especially?"

"Lambing tents most of all," Tom replied, "and jackets."

"J-jackets?" Rusty questioned.

"Yeh," Ben explained. "Canvas jackets we put on the lambs to keep 'em warm if the weather gets bad."

"I have a list of groceries written out," Tom Comfort went on. "There it is on the table. Send an extra blanket or two, if Rusty's going to stay. I won't have time to wash the one I loaned the ewe until lambing is over."

"I wish you could send Pal with the truck," Rusty said wistfully. "I'd like awfully well to have him here with me. And he could start learning how to be a sheep dog."

"I'll try," Ben said in a doubtful tone. "But don't count on it. He won't have much to do with me, you know. Or anyone but you. And he might not care about riding in a truck."

"Most likely not," Rusty sighed. "I'm afraid he'll be lonesome for me. Tell him I haven't forgotten him."

"I'll see that he gets fed," Ginger promised.

The twins got on their horses. Tom Comfort handed the bum lamb up to Ginger. She tucked it carefully under one arm, and they rode away.

V

Shepherd for a Night

"Want to help me bed down the sheep?" Tom Comfort asked.

"Sh-sure!" Rusty said eagerly.

The sun was sinking low behind the hills, casting a rosy glow over the world. The tinkling bells were hushed. The baaing was dying down.

Tom Comfort got on his black horse and Rusty climbed aboard Toby. They rode side by side without talking. Rusty noticed that the two black-and-white dogs were alertly taking care of the flock.

"You ride in one direction," the herder said. "I'll ride in the other. Just circle the flock. The dogs will help. I always try to get the sheep to bed down with their heads facing toward the center of the group. That way, coyotes and other varmints can't get at their throats so easy. If you notice a ewe in distress, wave to me. Don't yell or you'll get the sheep excited."

Rusty noticed that both dogs were watching Tom. He gave a large sweeping gesture with his right arm, and the larger dog bounded off to circle the flock clockwise. A similar gesture with his left arm sent the other dog in the opposite direction. Rusty, too, watched Tom, to see how fast he was riding, and how far from the sheep.

A feeling of peace entered Rusty's soul. The soft spring air, the gentle sounds of evening, the feeling that he was performing a helpful service, the beauty of the white sheep spread over the landscape—all gave him a sense of serenity and happiness such as he had never had before in all his life.

Somewhere he had read a poem in which there was the line, "All's right with the world." The line kept repeating itself over and over in his mind.

Tom was taking a slow gait. It was one which suited Rusty's mood. It pleased him to notice how intelligent the dogs were. Their heads up, they seemed to be looking over the entire flock to see if any were missing.

Suddenly the older dog seemed to become uneasy. He ran back and forth, looking at the woolly backs. He raised his head and seemed to be sniffing the air. He turned and ran into some bushes. There were two staccato barks, then silence.

Soon three ewes came out from the bushes, one followed by a knobby-kneed lamb. Rusty smiled. "Now how on earth did Jack know that three sheep were missing?" he said aloud. "They all look alike to me. Maybe Tom Comfort was right. Maybe Jack can count."

A few minutes later Rusty saw a ewe lying on the ground, her feet sticking straight up in the air. At first he thought she was dead, else she would have been struggling. But no; her feet moved a bit. Uncertain what to do, he waved his arm as a signal to the herder. Jack saw the signal, too, and came running up. He barked sharply a time or two, looking toward his master and ignoring Rusty, the newcomer.

Tom came trotting up. He dismounted hastily and rolled the ewe over and to her feet. She stood for a few moments, breathing hard, then commenced grazing.

"It's a good thing you noticed her," the herder said. "She wouldn't have lasted much longer. Once a sheep gets on her back, she's completely helpless. She can't get on her feet without help. And fifteen minutes is enough to kill her. She begins to bloat; the gas presses on her heart and lungs and kills her quick. That's one of the things you'll have to watch for."

"I-I'll know what to do next time," Rusty said apologetically.

"Oh, you'll learn," Tom Comfort told him. "Most folks think there's nothing to tending sheep but sitting on a hilltop and whittling sticks. They'd be surprised."

The slow circling of the flock continued. A few at a time, the sheep bedded down. Others continued to graze. Rusty noticed that most of them had their heads turned to the center of the bunch. When they were headed outward or strayed away from the band, the dogs gently but firmly nudged them back into the herd.

As dusk deepened, more and more sheep bedded down. When the circle was completed and Rusty and Tom met at their starting point, the herder said, "They'll be all right now. We'll go and get supper."

The two dogs followed at the heels of the horses.

"I have a b-black-and-white d-dog that looks a lot like Jack and that other dog," Rusty said. He went on to tell Tom of the wild dog and of how he had finally made friends with Pal and hoped to be able to train him to work sheep.

Tom shook his head doubtfully. "A dog that's had its spirit broken is usually ruined for good," he said. "It's almost impossible ever to build up its self-confidence again. Border collies are so sensitive that they have to be handled carefully."

"P-Pal is sensitive," Rusty nodded. "But he's so smart I'm sure he can be retrained."

"I hope you're right," Tom said as they reached the wagon. "We could use another good sheep dog or two around here. I'm having Socks work with Jack to train for another herder. I like to have two dogs with a herd. But not more than two. They want to play."

"I-I hope I can stay out and learn how to work sheep— and h-how to train sheep dogs," Rusty said earnestly.

He did not say how eagerly he hoped to be able to stay on at the Ram's Horn Ranch. Nor did he tell how often he awoke in a cold sweat at night from dreaming that someone had ridden up to the ranch to take him away. With each passing day his fears subsided a little. And out here, so far from people, he seemed safer than at the ranch.

They dismounted by the wagon and removed the saddles from the horses.

"Maybe you'd better hobble your horse," Tom said. He handed Rusty a leather strap from a hook near the door. "My horse will graze near the wagon, but yours might take a notion to hike back to the ranch."

Rusty stooped and fastened the hobble around the front legs of Toby. Then he gave the horse an affectionate pat on the rump. "Old boy! This is really living, isn't it?" he said.

He stepped upon the tongue of the wagon and entered the open door, which was divided into two halves, with panes of glass in the upper portion. He noticed that Tom pulled the lower half shut. "To keep out floor drafts," he explained.

Inside, the sheep wagon was a model of convenience. The small cookstove was near the door. Over it was a set of shelves for dishes and food. Benches were along each side. In the middle of each bench was a trap door opening into grub boxes which hung in the spaces between the wheels. The built-in bunk ran crosswise of the end of the wagon, with a window above. Fastened to the bed and jutting out between the benches was a hinged table. It was supported at the front end by a folding leg so it could be let down against the bunk when not in use. Beneath the bunk was a deep drawer.

Rusty fastened the hobble around Toby's front legs

"You can go out and chop some kindling and bring in wood," Tom said. "I've got enough spuds to warm up and it won't take long to fry the meat. Supper will be ready in the shake of a lamb's tail. A sheepherder's grub isn't fancy, but it's nourishing, and there's plenty of it."

The dogs lay outside, their heads on their paws. Their eyes were wide and alert. Rusty quickly chopped the kindling and carried the wood inside until the box by the stove was overflowing. Good smells of food filled the cozy sheep wagon.

Rusty perched on the edge of the bunk, watching Tom's deft movements. What a comfortable way to live! Everything was so snug. Merely by turning, Tom could reach everything he needed. The double canvas top, Tom told him, kept the place cool in summer and warm in winter.

"The wagon heats up kind of quick," Tom explained. "In summer that isn't so good. But with the door and the window open it cools off in a hurry. And in winter it's mighty pleasant to have the wagon heat up about as quick as you put a match to the wood."

He reached over and snapped on the radio. "We might as well tune in on the world," he said. "Though for the most part I'm well content to have the world and its hurry and flurry and fuss and muss stay far away."

Rusty nodded understandingly.

"It's nice to have someone to talk to, though, once in a while," Tom went on.

"I'm—I'm not much of a talker," Rusty said apologetically to the sheepherder.

"That's fine," Tom said. "I won't have a gabby person around. Sometimes I feel like talking, but mostly I don't. And I haven't any use for a person who likes to talk just to air his tonsils."

"It must get pretty lonesome here sometimes," Rusty put in.

Tom shook his head. "Oh, I suppose it would for people who can't stand their own company. But me, I like mine. I read and think a lot and I can't stand being around people very long. Some folks are unkind enough to say that a sheepherder is either crazy to start with or gets crazy before very long. Maybe so, but if that's the case, I sure enjoy being crazy."

Rusty smiled and relaxed. He liked Tom Comfort! He felt as though he had known him always and as though each understood what was in the other's mind.

Tom put some dishes on the table. "Slide over here on the bench," he invited. He put a plate before Rusty, filled with meat stew, fried potatoes, and canned tomatoes. Rusty refilled his plate and ate until he was uncomfortable. And then he had two helpings of canned peaches for dessert. It was plain food, but never had he eaten a meal which tasted so good.

The dogs were given the scraps and a can of dog food besides.

"I wish Pal was here," Rusty said wistfully when he saw Jack and Socks thrusting their noses into Tom's hand for petting. "He and I were just beginning to get well acquainted."

"He won't forget you," Tom said. "Maybe the kids'll bring him in the truck tomorrow."

"I don't think so," Rusty said. "He won't have much to do with anyone else."

He noticed that Tom had gotten out several round objects from a box under the sheep wagon. "You can help me carry these," he said, handing two of them to Rusty.

"They look like the f-flares they use when a truck stops in the road at night," Rusty said.

"That's exactly what they are," Tom nodded.

"B-but you don't have much traffic here!" Rusty exclaimed.

"The traffic in coyotes is quite heavy," Tom said gravely. "Especially at this time of year. There isn't anything a coyote loves better'n newborn lamb. But coyotes haven't any love for man or any of his works. So during lambing season we set out flares to fool the varmints into thinking that man is on guard."

Tom and Rusty set the flares around on the hills circling the bedding ground and lighted them. Rusty was very sure that no wild animal would dare venture within that bright circle.

"You can bunk in with me tonight," Tom said when they went back to the wagon. "There's room. But when they bring more blankets, I won't blame you for sleeping out—or under the wagon if you want to. That is, if the boss lets you stay with me."

"Oh, I hope he does!" Rusty cried. With all his heart he wished it. He felt so easy with Tom. And he had noticed that he hardly tightened up and stammered at all when he talked to the sheepherder.

Tending sheep seemed to him a wonderful occupation. He wanted to learn what a sheepherder had to do. If only he could make himself valuable enough on the Ram's Horn Ranch, perhaps he would be allowed to stay. He tried to close his mind on the wish, so that he would not be disappointed. But the desire was so great that it would not be crowded out. It was very big indeed in Rusty's heart as he went to sleep on the wide bunk beside Tom Comfort.

VI

"Sheep Are Dopes"

The rattling of the stove lid awoke Rusty. It seemed to him that he had just fallen asleep. The sun was beginning to tinge the world with pink, but Tom Comfort was already getting breakfast.

"Wake up, sleepyhead," he said. "I feel in my bones that this'll be a busy day."

"Ho hum!" Rusty yawned. "Nights hurry past awfully fast in a sheep wagon."

"You might as well get used to short rations of sleep until lambing is over," Tom told him. "We'll hurry now and grab some breakfast. The sheep always start moving as soon as it's daylight. At noon you can come in and cook up something to eat—just open a can or two. We'll take turns eating lunch. I hope the boss sends out more men today."

They were just finishing their fried eggs and hot cakes when a truck drove up. Willie, the man with the crooked nose and scarred lip, was driving. Ben sat beside him.

"Dad'll send out another man tomorrow," Ben said breathlessly. "That is, if he can get anyone from town. He said I could stay and help today."

Tom did not look too delighted. "One kid, if he knows how to handle sheep, can help a lot. But two kids are worse than none," he said curtly.

Ben gave Rusty a wink. "Maybe we can change your mind about that."

"You can't drive the truck," Tom said. "And I'll need Willie every minute."

"I can drive the truck," Rusty spoke up. "I've done a lot of driving across prairies."

"I'd want to get the boss's O.K. on that," Tom said doubtfully. "You aren't much older than Ben."

"Honest to g-gosh!" Rusty protested eagerly. "I'm a good driver."

"There'll be plenty for you to do," Tom said. "Hop in, everyone. Drive close to the flock, Willie. We'll see how things went last night."

The truck went bumping over the prairie.

The sheep had left the bed ground and were spread out over the valley and hillside. Several lambs had been born during the night. They were ugly creatures, already changed from their original tomato color to a dirty looking brown. Their scraggly legs looked unsteady and too long for their bodies. Their skins fitted loosely and hung in great wrinkles, making them look as if they had by mistake gotten into someone else's clothes which were too large. They were wandering around, baaing pitifully, and seemed lost from their mothers.

"Ho! Trouble has started," Tom said. "Every year at lambing time I get stuck with a band of two-year-olds. Too young and giddy to take their responsibilities seriously."

"You're the best herder Dad has," Ben told him. "That's why you always get the hardest job."

Tom paid no attention to the compliment. His attention was on something else.

"Drive over by that rock," he directed Willie. "Something's wrong!"

Rusty stretched his neck. He saw something white beside the rock—as if a ewe were down, but he could not see what was amiss.

When they drove up alongside the rock, a cry of horror came from everyone. There lay three ewes and a newborn lamb, all with bloody throats.

"Coyotes!" Ben exclaimed.

They all jumped down from the truck and stared at the gruesome sight. Tom pursed his lips and shook his head. " 'Twasn't coyotes," he said. "I had flares out. They wouldn't come near the herd. And the dogs didn't bark. There wasn't a sound all night."

"This is kinda off from the bedding ground," Ben pointed out. "Maybe the ewes wandered over here and the coyotes grabbed 'em."

Willie shook his head. "I agree with Tom," he said.

"This job was done by a sheep-killing dog. A lot of ranchers have been bothered the last few months. Coyotes and dogs do the same sort of job. Slit the throats with their teeth."

"Gosh!" Ben cried. "Two of those ewes were about to lamb. That makes six sheep that Dad lost last night."

"Hey you, Jack and Socks!" Tom pointed at the dead sheep, his voice accusing. "Why didn't you take care of these? Can't you smell and hear? What do I keep you for?"

Rusty felt sorry for the two dogs. They acted as if they knew what was being said. They hung their heads and crept along on their bellies to Tom, as though begging his forgiveness.

"All right." He patted their heads. "Don't let it happen again. You must take care of the sheep. Do so now. Round up any that are missing."

To Rusty's amazement the two dogs jumped up and went in opposite directions. They searched in each clump of bushes and sagebrush and behind every rock within the bedding ground and along the direction in which the sheep were feeding. Rusty thought that these truly remarkable creatures seemed to possess almost human intelligence.

"You boys can set up the little tents here and there," Tom said. "Some of these giddy ladies will have to be taught their duties. Rusty, you keep your eyes open and watch us. No one will have time to show you how to do this work, but right now we sure need all the help we can get."

Tom and Willie each took a shepherd's crook—a long wooden pole with a narrow hook at the end—and set out

to follow the herd. Ben thrust a piece of canvas into Rusty's hand. "Watch me," he said as he quickly set up a small canvas tepee.

"That's easy!" Rusty ran to erect his play-sized tent some distance away. Willie came toward him, using his crook to drag along a reluctant mother by a hind foot. Under his arm he had a small lamb. He shoved the ewe inside Rusty's tepee and held her down. Then he thrust the lamb's nose against one of her teats. She baaed a loud protest and tried to struggle to her feet. Willie held her firmly but gently. Instinct did the rest. As his stomach filled, the lamb's tail jerked with ecstasy. Finally the ewe relaxed and turned to smell the little fellow.

"That's a good girl," Willie said approvingly as he closed and fastened the tepee. "I'll give you a few hours together to get acquainted."

"I always thought any mother would take care of its young," Rusty said. "C-cows and h-horses and dogs and c-cats always seem tickled to death with their families."

"Sheep are dopes that way," Ben said. "The older ones aren't so bad, but a lot of these young ones that are having their first lambs have to be taught how mothers should act." He saw Rusty's interest and went on, "Sometimes, if a lamb lies down to take a nap, its mother will walk along, eating grass. Then, when the little fellow wakes up, he's lost for sure. That's what makes lambing time such a nightmare. We have the dickens of a time pairing up the lambs and their mothers. But after they get used to each other, each of them can find the other out of the whole flock."

"It makes me l-laugh to see Willie so gentle with the sheep," Rusty said. "He looks so mean."

"He's as kind as they come," Ben explained. "He got his face cut up in a car accident. Dad says he's the gentlest hand with lambs that he has."

Rusty and Ben ran along, quickly putting up their tents wherever the two men signaled that they wanted them. Now and then they stopped to teach some ewe her duties to a wailing lamb running after her, or to try to find the right mother for some piteously bleating little fellow who was lost.

Rusty picked up one lamb and tried to put it to suckle at a ewe who was near. She refused to have anything to do with it. Rusty left to help out another lost lamb, leaving this situation for more experienced hands. Ben burst out laughing.

"That lamb thinks you're his mother," he giggled.

Rusty turned. Sure enough, the little fellow was running up to him, bleating piteously enough to soften a heart of stone.

"That old lady w-won't have anything to do with him," Rusty said. "What do I do now?"

"Hey, Tom!" Ben called. "Here's a sure-enough orphan. His mamma has forgotten she had a baby. Or else we didn't find the right mother. He won't last long if he doesn't get some nourishment. His coat fits him awfully loose."

"Bring him over," Tom called.

Rusty followed to see what would happen. Tom was standing beside a ewe whose dead lamb lay on the ground. She was nosing it and baaing sadly.

"He's going to jacket your lamb," Ben said to Rusty. "Watch. This is interesting."

Tom had his pocketknife in his hand. He picked up the dead lamb. The eyes of the mother blazed. She snorted and stamped her feet and made for the herder with lowered head. He merely shoved her away with his foot. The boys laughed at the ridiculous sight of the ewe charging the man.

Rusty watched Tom slit the hindquarters of the dead lamb, then peel off the hide as easily as if he were removing a sweater. He shook it right side out again and cut off the forelegs several inches from the body. Then he slit the hind legs. He took the orphan from Rusty's arms, thrust its hind legs into the slits, its head through the neck, and its forelegs into the short sleeves he had left. Then he placed the creature beside the ewe.

Rusty roared with laughter at the sight of the ragged hide around the small head, the two tails dangling. The jacket fitted quite smoothly.

The lamb tried to suckle, but the ewe snorted, ran a few steps, and looked around ferociously.

"Come now, old lady," Tom said, thrusting out his crook and catching her by the hind leg. "You want a baby. Here's one that smells just like your own."

He picked up the lamb and thrust it under her nose. The boys roared again at the bewildered expression on her face. Tom put the lamb beside her. Once more she sniffed it. The lamb was nosing around, searching for nourishment. When he found it, he sank to his knees. His own tail bobbed joyously while the spare tail hung limp. The ewe sniffed once again. Then, in her throat, she made that wonderful sound of contented motherhood which Rusty was to hear so many times during lambing.

"I didn't have any idea lambing was so interesting," Rusty said, as he and Ben went back to work.

"It *is* interesting," Ben agreed. "And it's fun, too. That is, it's fun at first. But a whole month of it gets pretty tiresome. You never know what a sheep is going to do next. Maybe that's why they're so interesting. A good sheepherder knows every sheep in his flock. I s'pose to you most of these ewes look alike. Well, to Tom each one is like a person. He says every ewe has a different personality."

Toward noon Tom sent the boys in to eat, one at a time, while the others worked. In the afternoon more tepees were set up and most of them occupied by a ewe and the lamb she was being made to accept. Then Tom set the two boys to herding the band of ewes which had lambed and were to be kept separate from the rest of the flock. These mothers had accepted their lambs and responsibilities. Some of the lambs were not yet certain to whom they belonged. They would run up to any ewe nearby when they were hungry. But the ewes indignantly walked off and refused to nurse any except their own offspring.

"It's k-kinda wonderful how things get born and right away know how to eat and where to get their milk," Rusty said thoughtfully.

Ben nodded. "I get a big kick out of lambing season," he said. "Every year it seems more wonderful. Then, with the air all full of spring smells—birds singing and grass green and trees popping out into leaf—gosh, it's mighty fine to be alive!"

Rusty nodded. That was the way he felt, too. His heart was warm and happy. Ben was swell. The Leonards were the finest people he had ever known. The whole world was just wonderful.

He sat on a hump of ground to watch his little band. Ben had gone over on the other side of the flock. Until Tom told him something else to do, Rusty thought he could take it easy, simply watching this small band. Just now things in it seemed pretty much under control.

He thought of Pal and wished he had the dog here with him so that he could start his training. He had meant to ask Ben why he hadn't brought the dog in the truck. He supposed it was because Pal wouldn't ride. He probably was frightened and jumped out.

Rusty stared up at the clouds, watching them lazily form their strange shapes. How serene and quiet the world was here! As if there weren't a trouble in the world.

He heard a sound behind him—a rustling in the bushes. Rusty turned, but there was nothing in sight. His skin prickled on his scalp. There must certainly be something there. Perhaps it was a wild animal.

Sternly he told himself not to be silly. A sheep or a lamb might be back there. He got up and walked toward the bush. He saw something black. Maybe it was a bear!

Then he heard a whimper. Rusty gave a startled jump. Again the whimper. Now the creature crawled forward on its belly.

"Pal!" Rusty cried. "How did you get here?"

The dog whimpered again. He put his forepaws against Rusty, whining his joy. Then Rusty backed away in horror. There were bloodstains on the ruff of white hair under Pal's chin! Rusty thought of the ewes and the lamb lying in pools of blood, with crimson-stained necks.

"But you couldn't! You couldn't!" he cried. "It couldn't be you." He refused to accept the horrible thought, yet he backed away from the dog's show of affection.

"I don't know what to do," he said aloud. "I don't know what to do. It wasn't you. I know it wasn't. But how did you get bloody?"

His reason told him that there were many ways in which an animal could get its neck bloodstained. It might have sniffed at the dead sheep. It might have got into a fight. It might have been attacked by a wild animal.

He led Pal to the stream and carefully washed the blood from his vest. His hands searched the black-and-white body for signs of wounds. But there were none. He had to discard the idea that Pal had been in a fight or had been attacked.

Rusty put his hands on the dog's head and looked deep into his eyes. "Are you going to ruin everything for me?" he asked. "I thought things were going just fine. Now this happens."

The dog gave a low whine which seemed to beg for friendship and trust.

"Oh, Pal, I know you couldn't do such a thing!" Rusty said. "But stay with me. Don't leave my sight."

VII

Where Is Pal?

Bruce Leonard came out that evening in a pickup with Ginger beside him. He was bringing two more men to help with the lambing. There was a supply of bedrolls in the pickup, for the crew would sleep right alongside the sheep bed ground.

The sheep wagon was moved closer to the bed ground. It would be used as headquarters for eating and for making coffee during the night. The work would go on ceaselessly now, with the crew members taking shifts.

Tom Comfort reported the finding of the dead sheep and the lamb.

"Coyotes?" Bruce Leonard asked.

"I don't think so," Tom said thoughtfully. "We had the flares out, circling the flock. Those generally keep the coyotes away. Besides, Jack and Socks always sound their alarm when coyotes are near. This looked to me like the work of a killer dog."

Rusty felt his heart shrivel up with fear. He glanced toward Pal, sprawled out with his head on his paws by the tongue of the wagon. Then Rusty jerked his glance away quickly, hoping that no one had noticed. He wanted to keep the minds of the men away from his dog.

"Coyotes are smart," the boss said. "They're probably learning that flares are harmless. I brought some firecrackers along. Set some off now and then. Keep fires going. Some of you will be moving among sheep all night. That should keep coyotes away."

Rusty heaved a sigh of relief. He was glad that the boss had not attached much importance to the idea of a killer dog.

"It's nice that Dad brought you along, Ginger," Ben said, grinning at his sister. "You can cook supper for us."

"Ho!" she said. "I s'pose you think I don't get enough of kitchen work at home. Peel potatoes, wash dishes, set and clear the table. It makes me so mad that you have all of the fun working outdoors while I have to slave inside."

"How's the b-bum lamb coming?" Rusty put in.

"Oh, just fine!" A sparkle came to Ginger's face. "He's a darling. Are there any more?"

"I have a black one for you to raise," Tom Comfort told her. "It's one of a pair of twins—the other is white. The mother owns the white one all right, but she seems to think it's a disgrace to have a black sheep in the family. She won't have it around, and I haven't found any other ewe who'll take it."

"Oh, I'd love to have a baa-baa black sheep!" Ginger clapped her hands.

"Remember the old Corriedale ewe we had a few years back?" Bruce Leonard said. "She had black lambs for three years in a row and was pretty proud of them. Then, when she had a white lamb, she disowned it and tried to steal other ewes' black babies."

Tom Comfort banged on the dishpan with a spoon. "Chow's ready!" he called. "Come and get it or I'll throw it out!"

"The men I brought have eaten," the boss said. "They can relieve Willie."

Since there was not room inside the wagon for everyone to sit, the men got in line. Ginger took her place along with them.

"They keep me so busy at the cookhouse, waiting on the men, that I don't have time to eat," she complained.

"There's plenty for you here." Tom Comfort smiled at her. "I expected you, so I made your favorite dish—son-of-a-gun stew. Everything's in it but the dishpan. Son-of-a-gun stew will be our main article of diet until lambing's done."

"It keeps getting better," Ginger told Rusty. "They add more stuff to it every day."

"Oh, about once a week they feed what's left to the dogs and start over again," Ben put in.

"Say!" He turned to Ginger as a thought struck him. "Did you remember to feed Pal? I put food out for him last

"Chow's ready! Come and get it!"

night. I was going to try to bring him out in the truck, but he didn't show up."

"I didn't see him," Ginger said, as she reached for a tin plate from the pile by the stove. She filled her plate with a generous portion of stew and three biscuits. The boys, who had already filled their plates, were on their way out to sit on the wagon tongue to eat.

Rusty had felt his face turn hot at the mention of Pal. He hoped his friends were so busy filling their plates that they had not noticed.

"Say!" Ben cried out. "Isn't that Pal right over there?"

"Sh-sh-sure." Rusty tried his best to sound casual, but he felt his face flush again, and his tongue tripped all over itself. "He-he's b-b-been around h-here."

"Did he find you all by himself?" Ben asked.

Rusty nodded, his face bent over his plate.

Ginger looked at him. "Well for goodness' sake! You don't need to blush over it," she said. "I think it was real smart of him."

Rusty could have kicked himself. Why must he act so stupid? Apparently it hadn't occurred to anyone to link Pal with the killing of the sheep. And there wasn't a chance in a million that he *was* connected with it. Then why should he, Rusty, act all covered with guilt?

"My!" Ginger exclaimed. "Pal's vest is so white. I never saw it so clean."

Again the hot blood rushed to Rusty's face, but this time no one noticed.

Willie came up and ate his supper. Then, because he

was the last one through, it fell to him to clean up the dishes. Rusty took pity on him and dried them, hurrying with the job so that he wouldn't miss anything outside.

When he left the wagon, the boss was lining up the duties for each worker. "Willie and Murphy take the shift until midnight," he said briskly. "Tom, you'd better get some rest. Then you and Walt take over."

He looked at Rusty. "Can you stay awake until midnight?" he asked.

"Sh-sh-sure!" Rusty said.

"Saddle your horse and ride slowly around the bedding ground to discourage prowling animals," the boss said. "But spend most of your time near the flock with the new lambs. Ben can put his bedroll near them. And keep one of the dogs close at hand."

A delicious shudder ran up Rusty's spine. This sounded exciting. Important, too. He would be helping to protect living things—and thousands of dollars' worth of the boss's property.

"I'm still shorthanded," Bruce Leonard went on. "Randy kindly condescended to ride back and forth on horseback, running errands and such, but he refuses to drive the tepee truck. Says that's a sheepherder's job. I told him he hasn't enough gumption to be a sheepherder."

"Rusty can drive a truck," Ben said with obvious pride in his friend's accomplishment.

"Yes," Rusty spoke up eagerly. "I've driven over all kinds of country."

"You're rather young," the boss said.

"I've done a lot of truck-driving though," Rusty repeated stoutly.

"Good. We may need your help." Mr. Leonard dropped the subject.

The men who were to have the first shift were already moving about the herd, doing whatever was necessary. Fires were blazing in several spots, for the night would be chilly. Dusk was settling over the land, and lanterns bobbed here and there.

"I put the box of firecrackers under the wagon," the boss told them. "Fill your pockets when you make your rounds on horseback. Once in a while set off a few to discourage any wild animals."

"I'll sh-sh-sure do that," Rusty promised earnestly. He was determined that while he was on duty no harm should come to Mr. Leonard's sheep.

Toby nickered softly as Rusty tightened the saddle girth.

"A lot depends on us," Rusty said in a low voice as he climbed into the saddle. He had filled his pockets with firecrackers and matches and carried a big lantern flashlight. He turned the light toward Pal, who sat watching him with an alert, eager expression. The dog whimpered, as though pleading to go along.

"All right," Rusty said. "Come along. But stay close to me." He jerked the reins.

Toby's hoofs made no sound on the soft grass. Rusty rode first to where the band of ewes with lambs was bedded. Ben was curled up in his bedroll, his feet toward the campfire. He stared up at Rusty.

"Good luck!" he said. "Don't go to sleep until after you wake me up. And that may be quite a job. Keep this fire going, and the other ones, too. And try to keep the sheep with their heads toward the center of the circle. And don't let the wolves get you."

It gave Rusty an eerie feeling to ride around the wide circle. There would be a full moon tonight. Before long he would not need his lantern flashlight. The blazing campfires, the men moving around with their lanterns bobbing, all appeared unearthly. Rusty fed the fires, flashed his light in all directions, and now and then fired off a bunch of firecrackers. Pal trotted at the horse's heels. Every time Rusty stopped, the dog came up beside him and gazed at his master with a gentle whimper, as if to ask if he could be of service.

"You're a good boy," Rusty told him. "I know you're good. You're my best friend. We're pals. I'm going to make a fine sheep dog of you. Together we'll make a pair that Mr. Leonard can't get along without."

Later, when the excitement of night sheepherding wore off, Rusty began to grow drowsy. At first he kept thinking that he heard strange sounds and believing that he saw eyes blazing from behind every stone and bush. Once Pal barked sharply and dashed off into the brush. There was a scurrying sound. Soon Pal came back. His bushy tail was erect and he looked quite proud of himself.

"Good boy! That's fine. Take care of the sheep," Rusty told him.

The dog almost twisted himself double in his delight over

the praise from his master. And Rusty got a warm feeling around his heart from such devotion.

At length time began to drag. Now the moon was full, casting its silver light over the world and giving it a ghostly look. Several times Rusty asked one of the men what time it was. Always he was surprised to find how slowly time was moving. And more than once he was awakened by the bobbing of his head as he dozed in the saddle. Each time he shook himself wider awake. When finally Willie called and told him that it was twelve o'clock, Rusty was very relieved to ride over to where Ben lay rolled up like a brown cocoon. He dismounted and shook Ben's shoulder.

"Go jump in the river!" Ben muttered sleepily.

"Get up. It's your turn," Rusty told him.

"Said jump in river before I push you in," the muttering went on. Ben's eyes remained shut tight.

"Come on then. Push me in. I dare you," Rusty laughed.

It took a good deal of shoving and pulling and prodding to get Ben awake, but at last the job was done.

As Ben was crawling from the blankets, Rusty took the lariat from the horse. He tied the rope around Pal's neck and to a nearby tree.

"Sorry to do this, old boy," he said. "It's just to keep you out of mischief until you learn what's expected of a good sheep dog."

Rusty yawned widely as he pulled off his shoes. This would be the extent of his undressing. He crawled into the still warm bedroll which Ben had vacated.

That was the last thing he remembered that night. When

he awakened the next morning, the red sun was streaming full in his face. He turned and looked for Pal. But the rope hung there, limp and empty, and the dog was gone!

Rusty leaped to his feet with an exclamation of alarm. He quickly washed his hands and face in the creek and hurried to the wagon. He was still a bit wild-eyed from his discovery. He looked around to see if Pal was in sight, but he was not. He wanted to ask if anyone had loosened him or had seen him, but he did not dare. He was relieved that no one reported any sheep killed during the night.

Rusty hurried to eat his stack of hot cakes. Then he saddled Toby and set out to circle one of the bands.

VIII

Excitement!

During the morning Randy galloped up on horseback. He looked for all the world like a movie hero with his wide hat, his blue gabardine shirt, red neckerchief, and fancy cowboy boots.

He came from the main ranch, delivering messages and mail to Tom Comfort. Then he rode over to see how Rusty was making out. He stared down at the boy with a teasing grin on his handsome face. "Don't let 'em make a sheep-herder out of you, my friend," the cowboy said. "I would never sink so low."

"I-I l-like to t-tend sheep." Rusty's voice had a tone of defiance to it. "I-I think it's interesting work. And it's f-fun t-too."

Randy's expression took on a tinge of pity. "That, my

dear boy, is because you've never tasted the delights of being a cowboy. You're inexperienced."

"I-I didn't say I w-wouldn't like to be a c-cowboy," Rusty said. "But I d-don't see why anyone should l-look down on sheepherders."

"Your ignorance is astonishing," Randy told him. "But don't let me discourage you. It just seems to me a fine boy like you is meant for better things."

"You didn't happen to see P-Pal at the ranch house, did you?" Rusty's tone was half fearful, half hopeful.

Randy shook his head. Then he gave the boy a questioning look. "I brought the mail in from town yesterday," he said. "And I couldn't help seeing that one of the letters to the boss has the return address of the sheriff's office."

Rusty's heart seemed to turn a complete flip-flop. "Yeh?" He tried to make his tone sound matter-of-fact.

"Yeh." Randy bore down on the word. "I just thought you might want to know."

"Why should I-I w-want to know?" Rusty bristled.

Randy shrugged. "Oh, I just had a hunch the message had something to do with you. I thought you might want to take a weight off your mind by telling Uncle Randy what sort of jam you were running away from. I might be able to help you out. I've been about quite a bit, you know."

"I-I see one of those f-fool ewes on her back over there," Rusty said hurriedly. "I've got to r-roll her over."

"O.K.," Randy said with a good-natured smile. His heels pressed his horse's sides. "I'll be seeing you."

When Rusty went to the wagon to get his lunch, he found

that Willie was taking his turn as cook. He had the son-of-
a-gun stew bubbling on the stove and the biscuits made.
He was sitting on the bench inside the wagon, holding a
bum lamb and feeding it from a bottle. Rusty wanted to
laugh at the sight. In spite of its ugliness, Willie's battered
face had a tender expression, and he held the lamb with
the gentleness of a mother.

The others came straggling in. They filled their tin plates
with food and went outside to eat.

Rusty was just getting up from the ground, where he had

been sitting, to take his plate inside to wash, when he saw Tom Comfort ride up. Rusty stopped in his tracks and gasped. For at the heels of the horse trotted Pal.

"Wh-where did you find P-Pal?" he gasped.

"Oh, he's been with me since early morning," Tom said. "He followed Jack over. Jack seems to have taken Pal in hand. He's been teaching your dog the tricks of tending sheep. And is Pal smart! You have the making of a wonderful sheep dog there, or my name isn't Tom Comfort."

Rusty's tin plate clattered to the ground. He rushed forward to throw his arms about the dog and to bury his face in the woolly neck. He was almost bawling with joy over Tom's words. Now it was not important how the dog had got loose—whether he had been untied by someone or had untied the knot with his own teeth. He had not been in trouble. And he did have the makings of a fine sheep dog!

Rusty did not know when he had been so happy. An enormous load was lifted from his shoulders. Pal was not a killer! He was a good sheep dog—and sheep dogs did not kill the creatures they tended.

The days rushed by. Rusty shoved into the back of his mind the news Randy had brought about the sheriff's letter. He told himself that it did not concern him.

He did a bit of everything—herded sheep, put up tents and built small corrals, ran the truck a bit, and even took his turn as cook. He never got enough sleep, but each morning, after he finally shook the grogginess from his senses and

97

got into the swing of the work, he did not mind. He was having a wonderful time.

The most wonderful thing about it was that Pal was developing into a fine work dog. He instinctively seemed to know what to do. He watched Jack perform and, under the wise guidance of Tom Comfort, Pal's instincts were receiving the best sort of direction.

At first Rusty was a bit jealous because Tom was able to handle Pal. He had hoped that Pal would be a one-man dog, with no other master than him. And eventually that was the way it proved to be. Pal would take orders from Tom, but he always looked about to see if Rusty nodded his approval. And it was to Rusty that he came for praise and affection.

Tom seemed to sense what was in Rusty's heart. One day when they were driving a flock to new pasture he said, "Pal has sense enough to know that you aren't boss of the outfit yet. He realizes that I'm directing things. That's why he looks to me for orders. But he's all your dog. He won't have anything to do with me when we're not working sheep."

Rusty smiled his gratitude for the herder's understanding words.

The first few times Bruce Leonard came to the sheep camp after Randy had told him of the letter from the sheriff, Rusty waited fearfully for the boss to say something. But as the days slipped by without anything being said, the feeling of dread eased from his mind.

At last lambing was over. There was a good lamb crop, the weather had been favorable, the ewes and lambs were in good condition, and everyone was happy.

Slowly the various bands which had been divided according to the ages of the lambs were being herded together again. They were driven to new pastures to graze until shearing time.

Rusty had hoped to be allowed to stay with Tom Comfort or one of the other herders to help tend one of the flocks, but he was taken back to the ranch to help there.

One of Rusty's chores was to fill with milk the round metal container with the twelve rubber spigots—the mechanical mother in the corral where the bum lambs were kept.

Mrs. Leonard suggested that Ben, Ginger, and Rusty each adopt three of the nine "bummers" as his or her own, to see who could raise the best lambs. Each took turns picking his three. Then each painted his initials on the lamb's rump with waterproof paint. At first the lambs all looked alike to Rusty, but soon he could pick his own out from the others. He noticed that they were developing distinctive personalities. He saw to it each day that his lambs got their share of milk and that they were kept clean and well.

But there was not too much time to play with the lambs, which were in a week or two as tame as dogs and would walk in and out of the cookhouse whenever they got a chance. Shearing time was almost here now, and everything must be ready so things would run smoothly.

The long sheds were cleaned and the fences and gates repaired. The hay in the loft of the big barn was smoothed. Some of the shearers would want to throw their bedrolls there, preferring this sort of bed to sleeping in a tent.

"Where do you get your shearers?" Rusty asked Ben. "Do the men who stay here do it?"

Ben looked disgusted with such ignorance. "Of course not," he said. "There are regular shearing crews who start working when spring first hits the south—about January. Then they work north. I've heard that in the warmer climates they shear the sheep late in the summer, too. But of course we just get one wool crop here."

"Isn't that good enough?" Rusty asked.

"Well," Ben agreed, "it's a pretty good business. The sheepman gets a lamb crop and a wool crop for each ewe. Cattlemen only get the calf crop."

"Is shearing as exciting as lambing?" Rusty asked.

"Yeh, I guess so. But in a different way. There's just as much of a rush, but we do get more sleep. The shearers only work an eight-hour day. No night shifts."

"That's good news," Rusty remarked.

"Dad's had the same crew for three years," Ben went on. "A crew's usually about fourteen men. Dad's is good. Each shearing crew elects its own captain. He's the boss and business manager. And of course all of the men on the place pitch in and help."

"I'll bet there's plenty to do," Rusty said.

Ben nodded. "Willie's an awfully good shearer," he told Rusty. "He always takes a blade and makes some extra money. He used to travel with a crew until he got banged up in the auto accident. He and Pablo, one of the traveling crew, usually have a shearing race. It makes things more exciting. There's a lot of rivalry between them."

At the supper table Rusty heard arguments over the respective merits of hand and machine shearing. He learned that many of the ranchers were turning to electric power machine shearing, because it was faster. Bruce Leonard, however, held out for the old way—shearing with hand shears.

"Machines shave the sheep, not clip them," he said. "If it turns cold, the poor sheep get chilled with nothing to protect their backs. Or if the sun shines they get blistered. And they don't have time to grow fleece long enough for winter protection. In time the quality of the wool drops after machine shearing. I like it that on this ranch sheep are tended by shepherds and sheared just as was done in Bible days."

"In those days," Melissa Leonard spoke up, "shepherds were respected and looked up to. Now, for some reason that I can't understand, it's cowboys who are clothed in glamor, and the shepherd is considered at the bottom of the social scale."

"But not at the bottom of the economic scale," her husband said. "Now sheepherders are paid a good wage and are given their living quarters and groceries. They earn more than cowboys. And, for my money, one good sheepherder is worth about five cowboys."

"You're prejudiced." His wife smiled at him. "You'd better not let Randy hear you talk like that."

A contemptuous snort was the only answer.

The shearing crew arrived one evening. Before nightfall

the place looked like a small village. Tents had sprouted around the ranch buildings. There were cars and trucks everywhere and men wandering all over the place.

Anxiously Bruce Leonard scanned the sky, hoping for clear weather. The baaing of sheep being bedded down was loud. Already the herd which would be first into the shearing pens was on the side of the hill, ready to be driven into the pens the first thing in the morning.

The men were up before daylight. Breakfast was ready, for Mrs. Leonard and Mrs. McAlester had been up since four o'clock. A very sleepy Ginger was there, too, passing the serving dishes. It was plain that everyone was expected to do his—and her—part.

The men hurried through the meal, and the shearers went to the whetstones and sharpened their shears. These looked like the clippers with which lawns were trimmed.

"You stay around the corrals," Bruce Leonard told Rusty. "Keep your eyes open, and you'll soon find out how to make yourself useful. There'll be plenty for you to do. The shearers and my men will keep you busy."

IX

Sheep-Shearing Contest

Already the first band had been driven into the large corral. The ewes were cut away from their lambs, who crowded the fences, bleating pitifully for comfort.

Soon the ewes were driven into a chute so narrow that only one at a time could pass. Rusty was handed a "dog"— a bunch of tin cans tied onto a wire. He was to haze the sheep into the chute by rattling this noisemaker.

The hubbub was continuous in the corrals and the shearing sheds. The ewes did not seem too concerned over being separated from their babies. At first they baaed, then stolidly accepted what lay in store for them.

They allowed themselves to be shoved from the corral through the chute and into the shearing pens where they waited patiently. There were two wranglers whose job it was to see that each shearer's pen held several sheep.

It amused Rusty to see the shearers lug the sheep about like big dogs. A shearer would take hold of one and prop it up on its haunches. Then, kneeling to the left of it, he held the ewe's underjaw with his left hand. In his right hand he gripped the clippers. Beginning at the neck, he sheared diagonally toward the breast, neatly finishing off row after row from the crease of the neck to the belly, then down to the rump and the tail. One side finished, he flopped the sheep about and clipped the other side. All the while the sheep sat like a bag of meal, only the eyes moving with a patient, long-suffering expression.

When the sheep was sheared, it was turned out into the chute leading into a pen. Now it was a scrawny, dirty, yellow creature, naked and ashamed looking.

The wool lay on the floor of the pen in a thick, unbroken fleece. A Mexican boy quickly seized it and deftly tied it into a bundle with a long cord. Then the tied fleece was thrown up to the stomper, standing inside a narrow, six-foot sack suspended from a frame.

Rusty looked up in wonder. Only the man's head was showing. Obviously it was this man's duty to pack the wool in tightly. It must be hot, dirty, smelly work, Rusty thought, especially while the man was working at the bottom. As the sack filled, of course he rose higher and higher. When the sack was full, the stomper sewed the top shut. It was released from its hangings, and two men rolled it outside and up an incline into a waiting truck.

The stomper signaled to Rusty to bring him the water

Rusty hazed the sheep into the chute by rattling a "dog"

bucket. When he was through drinking, and while the next sack was being fastened in place, Rusty asked a few questions to satisfy his curiosity. He was told that the fleeces weighed between seven and eight pounds, and that the long, narrow sacks, when full, weighed from three hundred and fifty to four hundred pounds.

Then the stomper swung himself up, hung to the frame until he had thrown a few fleeces into the new sack, then disappeared inside.

"Whew!" Rusty exclaimed aloud, to no one in particular, "that's one job I wouldn't care for."

"He gets paid time and a half," Ben said as he hurried by, rattling his tin-can dog.

"When will Willie and Pablo start their contest?" Rusty asked.

"Tomorrow, I think," Ben said. "They're getting warmed up today."

By noon the large corral was filled with scrawny yellow creatures. The lambs in the adjoining corral for the most part had finally ceased calling their mothers and had bunched together for comfort. But now hunger was making them raise their voices in loud complaint again, and the mothers crowded against the bars of the fence, adding their voices to the clamor.

Ben ran to swing open the wide gate between the two corrals. "Watch the mothering-up," he called to Rusty. "It's fun."

Fun, Rusty decided a little later, was not the word for it. Miracle would have described it better. Several hundred

shorn ewes were in one corral. Then, as soon as the gate
was open, the lambs poured through like white floodwaters.
The ewes ran to meet them, their heads up, worried ex-
pressions in their eyes. The bleating was deafening. Lambs
ran here and there searching, trying out various fountains
of nourishment. But now the mothers would not be fooled.
Rusty could not see how the mess ever would get straightened out. Certainly the lambs could not recognize these
scrawny, yellowish creatures as their mothers! And he remembered how reluctant some of the sheep had been at
first to accept their own lambs. How could this mix-up ever
be unscrambled?

But now a number of lambs had found their right mothers. There was no doubt about it. The mothers bleated with
content as contact was established. The lambs fell to their
front knees and their tails bobbed happily as the warm
fluid flowed into their empty stomachs.

Most of the sheep and lambs, however, were still searching frenziedly. Rusty ached to be able to help them get
straightened out, but he could not identify any of them.
There would surely be a lot of unmatched mothers and
babies left, he thought as he walked toward the cookhouse
for dinner. Probably the tenting and corraling job would
have to be done all over again, and the mothers tricked
into accepting other offspring than their own.

But to Rusty's surprise, when he returned from lunch, the
mothering-up was completed. Every ewe had her own lamb,
and all were being turned out of the corral and spread out
over the low hills like flowing water.

The shearing contest between Willie and his rival Pablo was to commence the next day. It was raining when Rusty awoke. He saw that none of the men in the bunkhouse were up, although some of them were stirring. Evidently there would be no shearing today.

Finally the men stretched and yawned and started dressing. "Can't they shear when it rains?" Rusty asked.

"They can't pack the wool when it's wet," Willie said. "It would mildew."

"And it takes about five hours of good hot sunshine to dry out a sheep's heavy coat," Mont added.

"I hope thees weather she clear off queek," Juan said. "Everyone he get so grumpy when she rain."

"Does the boss have to pay the shearers when they don't work?" Rusty asked.

"Not the shearers. They get paid by the number of fleeces they shear. But they eat just as much when they're idle as when they're earning twenty or thirty dollars a day," the foreman explained.

"Which is rather hard on the boss's pocketbook," Walt added.

"And it's just as hard on the women who have to do the cooking," Willie observed. "I think they hate rainy weather more than the men do. They have just that much more hard work to do."

It rained for three days, and with every hour of leaden skies and chilling rains the shearing crew became more dissatisfied.

The men seemed to think that over the next hill the sun

must be shining, and that they would lose out on several jobs unless it cleared. It seemed as if they partly blamed Mr. Leonard for the foul weather.

Rusty felt sorry for the shorn sheep. Without their warm coats to protect them they must be feeling the cold.

"There's a lot of grease in that half inch of wool that's left from hand shearing," Ben told him. "I don't think a thick coat of wet wool keeps them very warm. What Dad's afraid of is that it might turn cold and start snowing. The lambs are big enough now so that most of them would pull through. But we always lose a lot in such weather, especially if it comes during lambing season."

One of the ranch dogs came up. Ben patted its head. "Where's Pal?" he asked. "I haven't seen him around all day."

"Oh, he's around somewhere." Rusty tried to sound casual. But he had been wondering the same thing himself. He did wish that the dog would stop wandering off. That seemed a very bad habit for a good sheep dog to have. And a very difficult one to break.

While they were eating the noon meal the telephone rang. Bruce Leonard answered. A frown puckered his brow as he listened. "I'll be on the lookout," he said. "Thanks for warning me."

"A sheep-killing dog is on the prowl again," he said briefly. "Got eight of Brewster's sheep last night."

"Anyone see the dog?" Walt inquired.

Rusty bent his head over his plate to hide his face.

"No," Bruce Leonard said shortly.

"You sheepherders better keep your rifles loaded," Walt remarked. "The only cure for sheepkilling in a dog is a dose of lead."

Rusty felt as if he had received a dose of lead in his heart, it felt that heavy. And suddenly his food tasted like straw and stuck in his throat.

That afternoon the sun came out. Everyone cheered up. Tomorrow the shearing could be resumed, and Willie and Pablo could have their contest.

That evening after supper Pal appeared at the door of the cookhouse. He waited to be fed along with the other dogs. He was wagging his tail and grinning for Rusty's approval. But the boy's hand did not reach out to pat the black-and-white head. As he stood looking down at the dog, his heart held a mixture of emotions. What was back of Pal's mysterious disappearances? Why had they occurred at the same time sheep had been killed? Was it his duty to tell the boss about the dog's disappearances?

He turned icy cold at this thought. He knew now that a dog which was even suspected of being a killer would not be put up with on a sheep ranch. But he was not sure that Pal was the killer. Even a dog should be allowed a fair trial and not be destroyed merely on suspicion. Besides, Pal was his best friend on earth, next to Toby. No. He could not say the word which would certainly spell his friend's doom. Until the dog was proved guilty he should be considered innocent.

In spite of his decision, Rusty was long in getting to sleep that night. He knew what he owed the boss—yet it was impossible for him to betray Pal.

Willie and Pablo had both sharpened their shears the night before. As soon as they had eaten their breakfast they hurried to the shearing pens.

Ben was given the responsible job of keeping tally. He gathered up the sheared fleeces and tied them in bundles with strong twine. Then for each fleece he placed a black mark on the tally card tacked beside each pen. Rusty was given the job of "dogging" the ewes from the chutes into the pens to be sheared, then out again after the job was completed. He tried to see that this part of the operation moved smoothly—the shearers became angry when they had to wait.

While he worked, Rusty kept his eye upon the two men who were racing. Willie's sheep might have been paralyzed, it was so docile. He propped it up on its haunches and leaned its back against his knees. The animal looked up into his face with a ridiculous imploring expression as if saying, "Oh, do not hurt me, kind sir! See! I trust you so much that I do not even struggle."

Then, *snip, snip, snip,* Willie plowed a strip straight down the animal's breast. When the wool billowed around his feet until he seemed to be standing in a cloud, Ben hurriedly gathered it up. Willie shoved the naked, scrawny animal away, and Rusty quickly pushed another one within his reach.

Ben came over and said to Rusty in a worried manner, "Pablo is half done with his second sheep. Willie's out of

practice. The Mexican will probably beat him.''

"Oh, I hope not," Rusty said.

Bruce Leonard, passing by, overheard them. "Wait and see," he remarked. "It isn't the morning's work that counts. It's the even, steady speed."

At noon both contestants were willing to leave their pens

for lunch and to relax for a time. Pablo was three sheep ahead. He was grinning in triumph, but Willie did not appear to be worried. One of the men passed a hat and each shearer contributed a dollar as prize money for the winner. This would be in addition to what he earned from shearing.

At one o'clock the shearing began again. Willie, as calm and unhurried as ever, cut wide, even furrows. Pablo flew at his sheep, and his motions were unsteady. Every now and then he had to go back and shear a patch he had missed. And not a single sheep left his pen that was not cut and bleeding.

Tom Comfort noticed what was going on and called Mr. Leonard's attention to it.

The boss strode over in a rage. "Hey, you Pablo! You can't win this contest at the expense of my sheep. I won't stand for such butchery."

Pablo shot him a sullen look, but he worked more carefully. By the middle of the afternoon, Willie was still snipping away with steady, even motions. Pablo was only a sheep and a half ahead of him now. As the afternoon wore on the motions of the Mexican became more unsteady, although he was being more careful not to nick the sheep so often. For a time he spurted ahead, making it appear that he would regain the ground he had lost. Then he slipped back again.

"He's getting tired," Ben whispered to Rusty. "Willie looks as if he could keep on forever."

Finally, with an angry roar, Pablo straightened up and

cast his shears away. "Pablo troo!" he shouted. "He tired. Geev up. My hand, she cramp."

But still Willie clipped on.

"Hey, Willie!" Ben cried. "You can stop. Pablo quit. You've won."

Willie gave Ben a quiet smile and went right on clipping. "Might as well do a day's work," he chuckled. And he went on shearing until six o'clock.

Rusty went around to the tally card, and he and Ben counted the score. Willie had sheared one hundred and fifty-nine ewes, making a record.

X

"Will I Stay?"

As soon as the ewes were sheared they were branded on the left hip with the RH of the Ram's Horn Ranch, with blue paint mixed with linseed oil. Rusty was told that this brand would grow out with the wool, and that it must be repeated in six months.

Later the ewes were dipped in a tank of disinfectant for the prevention of scab, ticks, and various other insects. Following this, the lamb's tails were cut off. After these activities the ranch settled down to a pleasant, unhurried, but busy summer.

Rusty thought that Bruce Leonard sometimes stared at him in a strange manner, but for the most part Rusty had lost the worries and the uneasiness which had plagued him. An air of peace brooded over the ranch.

For a while, after the busy season ended, Rusty feared that Bruce Leonard would let him go. But as the shearers and extra help left and nothing was said to him, he relaxed. He tried hard to make himself so useful that the boss would want to keep him. He liked everything about the Ram's Horn—the sort of work he was doing, the beauty of the Colorado country, and especially the people. He had begun to feel at home, and at times almost as if he belonged. He seldom stuttered now, as he had little of the nervous tension which had sometimes seemed to tie him in knots.

When there was nothing special for Rusty to do about the ranch headquarters, he rode out on Toby to help one of the herders—usually Tom Comfort.

"I like to have an extra hand who knows how to tend a band of sheep," Bruce Leonard told him. "Sometimes a herder gets a toothache and has to be rushed to town. It's amazing how often sheepherders get the toothache," he said with a smile twisting the corner of his mouth.

"I-I'd like to take charge of a herd whenever you need me!" Rusty cried eagerly.

"It would have to be an emergency," the boss said. "You're pretty young. But anyway, learn all that you can from Tom. The knowledge won't hurt you any, and you never know what's going to turn up. You know, a herder has a big responsibility on his shoulders. Most of the time he's alone with a flock worth a great deal of money. And there are dozens of things that can go wrong. I've been fortunate in having herders who've been wonderfully loyal

"Learn all you can from Tom," the boss said

to my best interests—and who have had good judgment besides."

Rusty looked up at him, his eyes saying that all of his loyalty, too, was for the boss. Finally he worked up courage enough to blurt, "Do-do you think you can give me a steady job?"

Mr. Leonard looked thoughtful. "That," he said slowly, "depends upon several things." He gave Rusty a penetrating look. "You don't happen to be ready to tell me about yourself, do you?"

He shot the question so quickly that Rusty was caught offguard. He felt his face turning hot under Bruce Leonard's gaze.

"Wh-what makes y-you think there's anything to-to tell?" he questioned, and felt like kicking himself because his tongue got all twisted again.

"There might not be much to tell," the boss said mildly. "Except that there must be some reason for making such a mystery of who you are. If you were a grown man, I wouldn't pry into your past. But since you're a boy of twelve, or thereabouts, I'd like to know something about you." Rusty dug his toe in the dirt and was silent. Bruce Leonard waited. When there was no reply, he shrugged and walked away.

Rusty, going around doing his chores, was bothered again. What about the letter Mr. Leonard had received from the sheriff? Evidently the sheriff had not found out about him. Or maybe he had, and the boss was just doing a bit of prying on his own responsibility. He had not said whether he intended to let Rusty stay on at the Ram's Horn. He had said that it depended. Depended upon what?

Rusty resolved that if it depended upon how hard he worked, Mr. Leonard would have no complaints.

He was happy the next day to be sent out to help Tom Comfort. When he was out on the range, his worries eased away. There everything was serene. It was enough to let each quiet day take care of itself. The future seemed not to matter when he was tending sheep.

The sheep were up and grazing by sunrise. The flock spread out at least a square mile. The lively lambs leaping about reminded Rusty of white popcorn on green grass. Gradually the large band divided into smaller bands, going in many directions. Black sheep were used as markers, one to each hundred sheep. By counting his markers a herder could tell at a glance if any considerable number were lost. Around and around through the various smaller bands Rusty and Tom Comfort wandered, seeing that all was well.

It pleased Rusty to know that such a weight of responsibility was on his shoulders, even though he did not carry it all alone. A herder, he thought, carried far more responsibility than a cowboy did. In his and Tom's charge were around thirty thousand dollars worth of property, which a wrong move could destroy.

"Good old Pal!" he said when the dog came to him now and then for a pat of approval. Pal was proving himself very teachable under Tom Comfort's guidance and with Jack's and Sock's example.

Toward noon the flock drowsed and the lambs, tired of bobbing around, lay down to nap. Then Tom and Rusty went to the wagon to eat. After lunch they were out again to circle the grazing ewes and playful lambs.

Toward evening Tom's soothing call rang out. *"Sooo-ooo-ooo,* sheep. *Ooo ba-aa. Sooo-ooo-ooo,* sheep."

The ewes recognized this as the signal to bed down. Peacefully, in their own good time, they made way to the bed ground and one by one lay down. The dogs gave them gentle nudges, to help them along.

It was a peaceful, blissful life, but full of activity, too. Rusty wished that the days could go on in this fashion forever.

But one day Ben came to the camp with Mont Brill and Ginger, bringing supplies and the news that soon the drive to the "high country" would commence.

"Every summer Dad drives the sheep to the summer feeding grounds in the Mosquito Range country," he told Rusty. "The last two summers I've gone along to help. Gosh, I hope Dad lets you go this year. It's like a long camping-out trip. There isn't anything more fun."

"I hope he does let me go," Rusty said wistfully. "It sounds wonderful."

"I'll try to use my influence with Dad," Ben said importantly. "It'd be fun to have another boy along."

Ginger tossed her head. "Since Rusty's been here, you haven't had much time for me."

"Quit crabbing," Ben told her. "Dad let you help trail last summer. I s'pose he will this summer, too."

"But he didn't let me stay up in camp," she pouted.

"Of course not. You're a girl," Ben said, as though that settled the matter.

Ginger wrinkled her nose at him and went into the wagon.

"I feel kinda sorry for girls," Ben said. "They don't seem to have half as much fun as boys. Ginger's really swell, but she doesn't have a chance to do as many exciting things as I do."

"Ginger *is* swell—for a girl," Rusty agreed. "G-golly, I hope I can go."

Ben must have used his influence with his father to good effect, Rusty thought. For, a few days later, when Bruce Leonard came to camp, he told Rusty that he was to help with the trail drive and to stay with the herd on the summer range.

XI

High Country

Everyone was up before daylight the day the sheep drive was to start. The two-ton truck was already loaded with blocks of salt for the sheep, and with groceries and tents.

Rusty, helping with the preparations, was in a dither of excitement. A glorious summer of camping out stretched before him. After the summer was over, his future might loom as a gigantic question mark, but he would not worry about that now.

The herders and camp tenders all set out on horseback, for the trip would be long. Rusty rode Toby. It pleased him and made him feel important to have both Toby and Pal along to perform valuable service. Pal was doing the work of a veteran sheep dog, but looking to him always for directions. He would work for the other men, but preferred to have Rusty give his arm signals or whistles. And he made friends with no one else.

The camp tenders started first. Their job was to locate the camping places and to get things ready for the herders when they arrived.

"The mountains where we are going," Ben told Rusty, "are just covered with old mining camps. Lots of times we camp in cabins, but when we make longer stops, we put up tents. I like that better. Most of the time, I just take my bedroll and sleep out under the stars."

"Oh, I wish I could stay there with you," Ginger said wistfully. "Why did I have to be a girl? Boys have all the fun."

"You're lots nicer than most girls," Rusty said. "I never used to like girls, but you have almost as much sense as most fellows."

Ginger gave him a pleased smile as she climbed into the truck.

After the camp tenders had gone ahead, the slow procession started toward the blue mountains. The sheep would be allowed to take their own time, grazing as they traveled. Six herders and four dogs would keep them from spreading too far.

By midmorning the truck overtook them and roared past. It was so loaded with supplies that Bruce Leonard was crowded behind the wheel with scarcely elbow room. Ginger, perched on the blocks of salt, waved at them.

Rusty and Ben followed the flock, riding ahead when any of the sheep straggled away. They did not talk much, but every time they came within sight of each other they both grinned happily. Neither of them would have missed this for the world.

"Where are we going?" Rusty asked Ben during one of their meetings.

Ben pointed. "Way up there past timber line," he said.

"I should think it would be poor pickings up there," Rusty said.

"That's where you're crazy," Ben told him. "Timber-line clover is so rich we have to keep the sheep on the move so they won't bloat. They come down in the fall fat as butter."

To Rusty, camp the first night was simply camping out. Supper was cooked over an open fire and the herders slept under the stars. It was such a pleasant experience that Rusty hoped it would be repeated every night.

All around them, at the beginning of their climb, lay the soft gray-green dwarf sage. It gave a pleasant tang to the air.

Up, up, they traveled, with the landscape growing more beautiful, until often Rusty felt his heart almost stop beating from the sheer wonder which lay before his eyes. Mountains rimmed them on every side. The ranges beyond rose in dazzling electric blue.

They passed through areas where cattle were already on the summer pasture. Rusty wondered if there would be trouble. He had heard of bloody feuds between cattlemen and sheepmen. But the cattle went right on grazing as the sheep were driven past. The cowboys eyed the herders without too much friendliness, but there was no shooting or even arguments.

Rusty remarked about this to Ben.

"Shucks!" Ben said. "I've heard my dad say that sheep and cattle are a lot like Jack Sprat and his wife. The cattle go along and graze first, but they can't crop the grass very close, because a cow has teeth only on its lower jaw. Sheep have two sets, so they can get the grass just about to the roots. Besides, cows won't eat weeds and sheep seem to like weeds better than grass."

One day they came in sight of a cluster of shacks and log cabins.

"A town!" Rusty cried in surprise.

"A ghost town," Ben corrected him. "A place where some prospectors expected to get rich." He pointed to a shaft running into the ground. Its timbers were rotting away, and the dirt from the abandoned mine lay like an orange-colored fan upon the gray earth.

"No one lives here," Ben went on. "The place was deserted years ago. So now the old buildings belong to anyone who uses them. See, there's our truck. Our sheep tender has set up headquarters in that log cabin over there—the one with smoke coming out of its chimmey."

Ginger was outside, waiting. The boys rode over, dismounted, and went inside. Ginger followed them. The place made a cozy dwelling, with a cookstove and shelves piled high with canned goods and sacks of provisions. The cracks between the logs had been chinked, and the walls were decorated with calendars yellowed with age.

"The sheep tender is sort of boss over the herders," Ben whispered to Rusty. The lanky tender was just outside, talking with the herders. "We'll have to move camp every three days," Ben said. "He has to take down and set up the little tents we'll live in. And keep us supplied with groceries and salt for the sheep. He'll ride in to Hilltown every other day and phone a report to Dad, and give his list of supplies for the truck line to bring out."

"How will he get supplies to us if we climb any higher?" Rusty asked, looking up at the sheer heights above timber line.

"Oh, he'll use a string of Rocky Mountain canaries," Ginger said brightly.

Rusty laughed. He knew she meant burros and that the *he-haw, he-haw* of their unlovely voices had given them that name.

Rusty was rather sorry to see Ginger wave good-by to them as they started their climb the next morning. She would return to the ranch in the truck. He could understand why she loved this out-of-door life. She was really a swell person, even if she was a girl—just the sort of sister he would like to have.

The third day they started up again. On, on, they climbed, mile after mile, past gigantic boulders, mountains clad with every shade of green, peaceful valleys, quiet forests. They passed gushing streams and wide pools made by beaver dams, in which fish jumped.

Rusty kept his mind and eyes open to learn all he could about taking care of sheep. There was a great deal to learn,

126

including a knowledge of botany, in order to keep the sheep from feeding upon poisonous weeds.

There were other dangers in this high country. There were more wild animals which prey upon sheep than in the lowlands. Every day some of the ewes or lambs wandered off into the pines or brush or among the great rocks.

The dogs sensed their responsibility. They carefully watched the slowly moving flock and kept the main herd and stragglers from harm. Rusty was proud that Pal caught on to this new duty with amazing quickness. He had a talent for knowing when one of the flock was missing and would take off into the underbrush and soon return, driving one or more stragglers.

Toby, too, did his part well. No matter how steep the climb, he was always willing to struggle on faithfully. Rusty knew that he was fortunate to have two such fine friends.

He couldn't help bragging a bit to Ben about Pal. "All he did," he said, "was to watch the other dogs. Right away he seemed to know that he ought to keep the woollies from straying. Do you s'pose dogs talk to each other?"

"Maybe," Ben said. The boys were afoot now, ambling behind the grazing sheep. There was plenty of time to walk together now and then, or even to sit on a rock in the warm sun and talk for a while.

"Tom," Ben went on, "says it's instinct. He claims that Border collies and other good breeds are born knowing what to do. Put them to herding sheep and it just comes natural to them to know what to do, even with very little training."

"They do learn from other dogs, too," Rusty said stubbornly. "I've seen Pal watch Jack and Socks and then try to do what they do. Only Pal does it better."

"Pal's a fine sheep dog," Ben agreed.

Later that evening the boys were lying on their stomachs beside a beaver pond. They hoped to see a beaver, but none of the wily creatures showed themselves.

"It's fun having another kid along," Ben said. "But you're sure hard to get acquainted with."

Rusty looked surprised. He felt as if he had known Ben for years. He took it for granted that his friend felt the same way about him.

"Yeh." Ben nodded in response to the question in Rusty's eyes. "I don't know any more about you than I did the first day I saw you. You're pretty quiet. But that isn't what I mean. Most any other kid would naturally tell something about himself—about his folks—where he came from—where he went to school. But you keep as mum as a mummy and make a great big mystery of yourself."

Rusty sat up and hugged his knees. At first a wave of anger rushed through him at Ben's prying, but he caught himself up. Why shouldn't Ben be curious about him? His never saying a word about his life before he came to the Ram's Horn must seem very strange.

"I w-wish you wouldn't t-talk about it," he said miserably. "I thought maybe your dad had found out all there is to know."

Ben nodded. "I think he has. But he's keeping it to himself. And doggone! I can't help being curious."

Rusty swallowed and gulped. He ought to confide in Ben. But the desire to keep bottled up within him the things he was striving to forget was too strong. "I-I—just can't tell you," he said. "I w-wish you wouldn't ask."

"O.K.!" Ben shrugged. "Go ahead and be the mystery kid, if you want to. I like you anyway."

It was the most wonderful summer Rusty had ever known. The cool, lofty mountains gave him of their strength and calm. There was time to fish in the crystal, icy streams, and the trout they caught and fried in bacon grease over an open campfire was the best food Rusty had ever tasted.

When the two boys had time to ride about, they explored some of the abandoned prospectors' tunnels. They pretended to find gold nuggets as big as their fists and made up tall tales of what they would do with the fortunes they had stumbled onto.

Best of all Rusty loved the quiet evenings when the wild animals came out of hiding and went for water or browsed in the open places. The deer would look at him curiously and unafraid.

Always there were the slate-gray, black-eyed camp birds and chipmunks and squirrels, and the rock chucks, saucy and daring, and the porcupines. These, Ben told him, no one must harm, because this creature was the only animal which man could run down and kill with a club in case he were lost and needed food.

Once, when it was the turn of Ben and Rusty to cook

supper, they caught some trout and were getting them
ready to fry. Rusty was by the stream, cleaning them. Ben
had cooked some bacon, which made a mouth-watering
odor on the air, and fried some pan bread in the grease. He
came to the stream and stooped down to get a kettle of
water for the coffee.

Suddenly Pal set up a terrific barking near the camp.
Both boys rushed to see what was wrong. They stopped
short in their tracks. There were a black bear and two cubs,
eating the bacon and pan bread!

The boys added their shouts to Pal's barking. The mother bear looked up. Rusty wondered what he would do if the bear charged. He had heard that mother bears with cubs were dangerous.

"Here, Pal! Here, Pal!" he shouted as the mother bear lunged at his dog.

Pal paid no attention to Rusty's calls. He continued to dash toward the bear, barking fiercely. He was agile and alert, jumping back every time the bear lunged and swiped at him.

Ben started to yell at the top of his lungs. He waved his arms and made mock charges toward the bear. Rusty followed his example. The mother bear looked at the noisy creatures with disgust and ambled off into the woods, her cubs at her heels. Pal rushed at them, barking to speed them on their way. When he came back, he looked quite proud of himself.

"Good boy!" Rusty patted his head. "Good boy! But don't get too close to those claws. I wouldn't want anything bad to happen to you."

XII

Why Was It Pal?

Rusty hated to have the summer end. The herders had called what they were doing work, but to Rusty it had not seemed like work at all. Rather, it was a long, glorious vacation—with pay. That was one of the most astonishing parts about it. He was not only having the best time he had ever had, but he was to get paid for it.

Of course there were times when he had to scramble through rocks, looking for strayed sheep. There were times when things went wrong and all hands had to work with every ounce of energy. But even that was fun. For the most part, though, wandering through the mountains, where every scene was one of breath-taking wonder, or sitting on the side of a hill, watching the flocks, soaking up the sun, and dreaming pleasant thoughts, was sheer bliss.

Already there was a tang in the late August air.

"We're going to have an early winter," Tom Comfort said as he sniffed the frostiness one morning. "We'd better be getting down to the lowlands before we get snowed in."

Rusty's heart was heavy as the camp tenders started packing up for winter and the flocks began their descent.

Here and there an aspen was already touched with gold, giving hint of frost. The crisp air sent blood rushing through the veins of man and beast. Everyone was in rare good spirits and full of zest as they set out—all but Rusty. As he jogged along on Toby, a feeling of dread hung over him.

What was in store for him when he reached the ranch? Ben and Ginger would go to school. But what would happen to him? Would he be sent back? He shuddered at the thought.

Rusty knew that Bruce Leonard was a man with a stern sense of duty. He would do what he considered right. From the hints which Randy and Ben had dropped, the boss must have some sort of information regarding his past. What would he do about it?

Oh, if only he could stay with the Leonards! The wish was so strong that it made a tight knot come in the pit of his stomach.

No one had ever taught him to pray. But every night, when Rusty stretched out on his blankets, he stared up at the stars and wished with all his might, in a sort of prayer: "Let me be good enough so that the Leonards will keep me. Show me the right things to do. I want so much to stay."

Rusty wondered if Pal sensed his worry. The dog seemed troubled and restless. Often he came to Rusty, whining softly and nuzzling his hand.

"What's the matter, boy?" Rusty asked Pal, patting his head. "Sometimes you seem to know what I'm thinking."

Each morning Rusty awoke depressed, but after he stirred about a bit he caught some of the others' zest.

Through Western Pass they traveled, past the black pinnacles to the hills of the lower country. As they moved downward, the sheep walked with that vigor which comes to all animals when they descend from a high altitude.

The flocks poured through the gates of the mountains like rushing waters. One night an early snow covered the ground. The next morning the sheep fell into marching file, no longer looking white as they did against green grass.

"Dark snakes on white cloth!" Ben shouted, waving an arm toward the sheep.

Rusty nodded. He was feeling pretty blue. There was more to it this morning than worrying about his future. Tom Comfort had found three lambs killed. They had been at the side of the flock where Rusty slept. He had not heard the disturbance. Pal had not barked; in fact, he was missing, and Rusty's calls and whistles failed to fetch him.

Walt glowered at Rusty during breakfast. "Looks funny to me," he said in a disagreeable tone, "that that cur of yours should turn up missing right after three lambs have been killed."

"Don't jump to conclusions, Walt," Tom Comfort snapped. "It might have been a coyote—a bear—a cougar."

"Bosh!" Walt said in contempt. "This wasn't the work of any of those varmints. Each has his special way of killing. I've seen the work of killer dogs, and this had all the earmarks."

"You could be mistaken," Tom said quietly.

Rusty gave Tom a look to express his thanks. But in spite of Tom's defense, Rusty thought he saw a worried look on the old sheepherder's face.

"P-Pal is a sheep dog," Rusty said stoutly. "B-Border collies never turn killer."

"Ho!" Walt scoffed. "Don't they though! There was something queer about Pal from the start. He was wild. You kids finally managed to tame him. And you taught him the motions of being a good sheep dog, I'll admit. But there's still that wild strain in him. You can't ever train that out of him."

"Pal didn't do it. H-he d-didn't do it," Rusty said miserably, a great lump rising in his throat.

"All I can say," Walt said, rising to his feet and fussing with the rifle strapped next to his saddle horn, "Pal had better keep out of my way. I've always said there's only one cure for a sheep-killing dog. That's a good dose of lead."

"I'm the boss herder here," Tom Comfort reminded him. I'll give the orders for any dog killing that goes on."

"Ho!" Walt's eyes narrowed. "Bruce Leonard happens to be my boss. When we started out, he gave orders to shoot any sort of animal that molested or killed sheep. I reckon that goes for dogs as well as varmints."

"My dad didn't mean for you to go around shooting dogs

136

until you're sure they're killers," Ben cried, his lips trembling with excitement. "If Pal is the killer, he'll have to be shot, of course. But don't go shooting until you're sure."

"How many sheep is your dad going to have to lose until we're sure?" Walt asked. "I've a hunch it'll cost him a plenty to let you kids have that half-wild animal for a pet. I should think you'd have your father's interests more at heart."

"I do have his interests at heart," Ben cried. "I said that Pal should be shot if he's the killer. But you don't know. You're—you're just—just shooting off your mouth." Ben was fairly sputtering with fury.

Walt grinned as he got into the saddle. "You're getting so that you stutter just like Rusty," he said in a disagreeable manner.

"Th-thanks f-for sticking up f-for P-Pal!" Rusty said to Ben. "Th-that d-darned W-Walt makes me s-so mad I could spit."

"Me too." Ben frowned. "I hope Dad fires him. But listen, Rusty. I hate to say this. I don't think Pal is the killer. But if it should turn out that he is—or even if it looks that way—you know what will happen, don't you?"

"Y-yes!" Rusty said unhappily.

They rode along at an easy pace, allowing the sheep to graze at will. In the afternoon Rusty saw a truck approaching. As it came nearer, he saw that Bruce Leonard was the driver. Beside him sat Ginger in her familiar bluejeans and plaid shirt.

It was good to see them. When the truck stopped near

the main herd, Rusty hurried up to speak to them. He stared at Ginger, surprised to be so glad to see a girl.

"Hi there!" She smiled at him in a friendly manner. "When you and Ben went to the high country I was kinda glad to have you go so that I could do as I pleased for a while. But it's going to be sorta nice to have you back."

Rusty expressed his pleasure at having her include him in her welcome home by nearly splitting his face open with a wide grin.

Ginger walked over to where her father was examining sheep, running his hands over them, kneading and patting their woolly sides in a businesslike manner. Rusty followed. To him, the sheep looked butter fat. He thought that the boss would be delighted with the fine condition of the flock. And he was—with reservations.

"They're fat," Mr. Leonard said briskly, "but soft. Give them a couple of weeks on the dwarf sage and cured grass of the low country and they'll be in great shape. Gentle them toward the ranch," he told Tom. "I'll keep in touch with you and send extra help to begin the cutting out. Altogether, I'm well pleased."

Rusty felt a rush of pride at those words. He had helped get and keep the Ram's Horn sheep in tiptop shape. It gave him a pleasant glow of accomplishment. Sheepherding was satisfying work, as well as fun.

The boss and Ginger stayed while the herders made camp. Mr. Leonard had brought steaks along—a rare treat —and loaves of homemade bread and cookies. After supper he and Ginger would return home.

Rusty squatted by the campfire, his tin plate on his knee

As he squatted by the campfire, with his tin plate of food on his knee, Rusty kept glancing at the boss. Now and then he thought the boss gave him a half-strange look. Ginger, too, stared at him with her head tipped to one side, as if studying him. Or was he only imagining it? The strange sense of dread which had been hanging over him deepened.

As they were carrying their plates to the dishpan, Ginger came close to Rusty and said in a low voice, "I know something I won't tell. A big surprise. You'd never guess."

"Shush!" Ben warned her. "You know Dad doesn't want us to tell him—yet."

Rusty's eyes widened in alarm.

"Don't look so scared." Ginger giggled. "It's something nice. Anyway, I guess you'll think it will be nice. Ben and I do."

"Will you be quiet?" Ben frowned at her. "You know there's nothing sure about it yet."

"But maybe if we wish hard enough, it will come true," Ginger said with a toss of her head.

Rusty wondered what they could be talking about.

Later everyone sat around the campfire and talked of doings at the ranch and of what had taken place in the high country.

The boss said that the price of lambs and wool was up . . . that Tom Hawkens, a rancher who had been seriously injured in an automobile accident near the Ram's Horn gate before Rusty came, was getting better and should soon be out of the hospital . . . that work had been started on a new shearing shed.

The brisk talk made Rusty almost forget his worries, even the mystery Ginger had hinted of—a mystery which seemed to concern him.

As the fire died down, the talk did, too. Now and then someone yawned. Bruce Leonard, who had been half reclining, propped on an elbow, straightened up. "Well, Ginger," he said, "I reckon we'd better start home and let these men bed down. They've been up since dawn."

The men were stretching lazily when a dreadful din broke out. A terrified baaing, a barking of dogs, a shrill yelp. Everyone leaped to his feet at once.

Rusty strained to see across the now milling flock in the direction of the commotion.

"I told you!" cried Walt with a snarl. "It's that dratted dog of Rusty's at the sheep again. I knew all the time it was Pal."

He seized his rifle, which was propped against his saddle, raised it to his shoulder, and strode off.

"Oh, n-n-no!" the anguished cry was wrung from Rusty's lips. He put his hands before his face. Everyone seemed frozen.

The rifle spat fire. There was a terrible cry, almost human. Then there was silence, save for the everlasting, senseless baaing of the sheep.

"I got him!" The triumph in Walt's voice raised such a wave of hatred in Rusty that for a moment it made him sick.

"It—it—w-wasn't P-Pal!" Rusty's voice trembled.

"I'm afraid it was, lad." Bruce Leonard put his strong

arm around Rusty's shoulder. His voice was soothing. "The other dogs are all accounted for, Tom says. It was a black-and-white—a Border collie—after the sheep. I saw him myself. He had to be shot."

Rusty turned and walked away so that no one could see his face.

"Pal! Pal!" he sobbed to himself. "Why did it have to be you—my good friend?"

XIII

A Ghost Dog?

It was a golden day, with clear sun and blue, blue skies.
There was a snap to the air which should have lent wings
to anyone's spirit. The herders made a special effort to
make conversation about small things, avoiding looking at
Rusty's swollen eyes or noticing his downcast manner.

Ben handed him a filled plate. With a murmured
"Thanks," Rusty sat on the ground and put a forkful of
scrambled eggs into his mouth. It took an almost super-
human effort to swallow.

He scraped most of the contents of his plate onto the
ground for the dogs. Then, with his face turned, he walked
away from camp. Behind a clump of bushes he threw himself onto the ground face down and gave himself up to
bitter unhappiness. Why, oh, why did it have to be Pal?

Why could it not have been some other dog?

"Move on! Move on!" Rusty heard Tom Comfort call the signal for the slow daily march to begin. Still he lay there. Let them go on without him. Let Bruce Leonard fire him. He did not care about anything now.

"Rusty! Rusty!" He heard Ben's anxious voice calling, then footsteps. "Rusty!" Ben stooped and put a soothing hand on his friend's shoulder. "Don't be like this. Please don't. I know how you feel. Once my favorite dog got killed. It was awful. I thought I'd never get over it. But come on. You'll feel better if you move around."

"Go away," Rusty muttered. How could Ben's loss of a favorite dog compare with his loss of Pal? Ben had a family —friends—a home. He, Rusty, had had nothing but Pal —and now the world was empty.

"Come on, fellow. Act like a man," Ben begged.

Rusty rose on his elbows and glared at Ben with reddened eyes. "Go away," he snarled. "Didn't you hear me? I said, *go away!*" His voice rose to a shrill cry.

Ben backed off, his eyes wide with hurt and bewilderment. Rusty put his head on his arms again to shut out the sight. He had hurt Ben, and he was glad. He'd like to hurt everyone in the world and make them suffer the way he was suffering. He hated, hated, hated every person living.

Rusty had no idea how long he lay there, wallowing in his emotions. Then—a rough tongue was licking his ear. There was a soft whine. Oh, why didn't they leave him alone! Now they were sending the dogs to make him move.

"Go 'way," he mumbled.

The whine was louder now, and the licking at his ear more persistent. There was something familiar about that whine. Slowly, unbelievingly, Rusty raised his head. His eyes grew wide. He gasped, then blinked. No, it was not a vision!

He reached over and grasped the dog in a bear hug. "It's you! It's my Pal! Oh, I knew you weren't the killer! I knew it all the time. Where were you?"

145

Whines—half of joy, half at protest over being squeezed so tightly—were the only response.

After a perfect frenzy of hugging and petting, Rusty finally calmed down enough to notice that Pal had patches of dried blood on his fur. He saw, too, that one ear was cruelly torn and that there was a long deep gash on the dog's nose.

"What happened?" Rusty was all concern now. "You've been in a fight with something. What was it?

"It doesn't matter," Rusty told the dog, now almost beside himself with excitement. "You're alive." Rusty leaped to his feet joyfully. "That's all that matters. Come. We must hurry to catch up with the others."

The pace of the flock was slow. Racing and waving his arms, Rusty had little regard of the danger of scattering the sheep. Tom Comfort came galloping toward him, shouting a warning.

Rusty slowed down, stopped shouting and waving his arms, and pointed to Pal. Rusty's eyes beamed. He was too happy to talk. All that he could do was to point and grin.

Tom's mouth dropped open.

"Well, I'm a something or other!" he gasped. "I could have sworn it was Pal that Walt shot." He pushed back his hat and rubbed his head in wonder.

Suddenly Rusty's spirits began to drop again. "M-maybe W-Walt just st-stunned him!" It was such a horrible idea that it made him shudder.

"Oh, no," Tom reassured Rusty. "Walt shot and killed the dog all right. He went over to make sure. Juan went with him. The dog was dead as a doornail, they both said."

"D-did they th-think it was P-Pal?" Rusty asked.

"They were sure of it," Tom said.

The other herders came up and goggled wide-eyed at Pal.

"It isn't! It can't be!" Walt cried.

"Eees it a ghost dog?" Juan gasped.

Pal sat on his haunches, looking around with a bright expression. He seemed to know that he was the center of the attention and was thoroughly enjoying some sort of triumph.

As everyone stood in a circle, staring at Pal, again the doubt came to Rusty's mind. It was still hard for him to accept the good fortune of Pal's appearance.

"Are you sh-sure you k-k-killed P-Pal?" he asked fearfully.

"I sure as shucks killed him or his twin," Walt said, stroking his chin. "Leastways he appeared awfully dead when Juan and I dragged his body off into the timber."

"I see, too," Juan nodded. "With my own eyes I see very dead dog."

"Juan, you and Willie take charge of the sheep," Tom Comfort said. "Ben and Rusty and Walt, get on your horses and we'll ride over to where you dragged the dog's body. We'll see whether Pal had a double or not."

"Please let it be that Pal had a double," Rusty begged silently. "Oh, please let it be that way! Don't have it be that Pal was only stunned. Then he will still be under suspicion and have to be shot."

When they got into the thin growth of timber, Walt took

the lead. He stopped his horse, and the rest rode up and sat, looking down at the body of a dog.

"Pal had a twin all right," Tom Comfort said.

Joy welled up in Rusty's heart. "He sure enough did, all right. He sure enough did."

Pal was walking about the body, sniffing gingerly, the fur on his back stiff.

Tom Comfort dismounted to examine the body more closely. "This might well have been Pal's brother," he said. "Looks like one out of the same litter. Practically the same markings, except that he hasn't the round white patch around his eye. I wonder what happened. I heard of one sheep dog going wild—turning killer. But never a Border collie. I wouldn't have believed it could happen."

"L-look!" Rusty shouted. "The dead dog's ears are torn —and there's a gash on his leg. I bet Pal tried to run him off."

"Anyway, Pal is safe." Ben's grin was as wide as Rusty's.

Walt glowered at them, still hating to be in the wrong. "There may still be a bad strain in the dog," he said. "If they are from the same litter, there probably is. You want to watch that dog and see that he doesn't turn killer, too."

Rusty and Ben laughed loudly. Tom Comfort, in his quieter way, joined them. Walt rode out ahead in a huff.

Rusty hurried to trail after the sheep. Pal was running ahead, then back again, almost turning himself inside out with joy.

It seemed to Rusty almost as if he were floating on air. Never had the sun shone so brightly. Never had his heart seemed so light and warm. The world was a wonderful place, and he loved everyone in it.

The sheep were pushed slowly toward the Ram's Horn sheds. They were allowed all the time they wished to graze and put on good solid flesh from the nutritious grass of the prairies.

The ewes and lambs were driven into the pastures near the sheds. Then the ewe lambs were separated from the wethers. Dividing two of these pastures was a long, narrow, low chute with a funnel-shaped entrance and exit. Into this chute the ewes were driven. Bruce Leonard stood midway and seized each one around the neck. With a deft motion he forced her mouth open. In an instant he was able to tell, by the condition of the mouth, whether to keep the ewe or send her to market. If the teeth were worn down, or if the ewe's lips were cracked or sore, it would be impossible to fatten her again.

"Ewes' mouths and teeth usually go bad," Ben told Rusty, "when they're between five and seven years. And if the lambs have badly shaped mouths, they can never be fattened. They'll be shipped, too."

The ewes with good mouths were driven into the right-hand pasture for future service as mothers and wool producers. Those who had lived their time were driven into the left pasture, soon to be shipped with the wether lambs.

Rusty was shaking his tin dog to haze the reluctant ewes into the corral when he became aware of eyes upon him. He turned and saw Randy, the rodeo rider, sitting on the top rail of the fence.

"Howdy!" Randy raised his hand in welcome.

"H-howdy yourself," Rusty grinned. His heart gave a lift at the sight of the handsome cowboy with his devil-may-care air. This young man had an exciting fascination about him. Rusty wished that he could look and act like Randy—that he could be a successful rodeo rider, winning prizes right and left and the applause and admiration of throngs of people. He could not imagine a more exciting occupation. No wonder Randy wore such a self-assured air. He knew that he was good. It was natural that he look the part.

The Big Question Mark

It was good to see sweet-faced Mrs. Leonard again and the plump cook, Nellie McAlester, and the others. Rusty was pleased that everyone seemed glad to see him. It was just like his idea of coming home after a long absence. But he forced himself to push such thoughts from his mind. After all, he told himself, this was not his home, no matter how much he longed to have things that way. There was no use of leaving himself open to further disappointment and heartache. He must cultivate a thick hide and be able to take whatever came to him.

There were several slack days before shipping. Tom Comfort and Juan drove the sheep which would be kept on the ranch to new feeding grounds. The other hands about the ranch did not have much to do.

Pal started after the sheep as they were being driven away, then looked back to see if his master were following. Rusty was sitting on a corral fence. Pal came running over to him, whined, ran a short distance toward the herd, then back again, as though reminding Rusty of his duty.

Bruce Leonard, walking from the corral to the house, stopped to watch the performance.

"P-Pal th-thinks I ought to be herding the sh-sheep," Rusty explained.

"Yes, I see," the boss answered. "He's doing his best to get you back on the job."

Rusty squirmed and twisted his shoulders. He hated like everything to ask what was sticking in his throat, but it had to be settled.

"D-do you w-want P-Pal to follow the sheep?" he asked fearfully. "He works for Tom Comfort pretty well. But if y-you s-send Pal out—I-I w-want to go, too."

Mr. Leonard looked up at Rusty shrewdly. "Pal is your dog," he said definitely. "I have a hunch you two need each other."

Relief flooded Rusty's heart. Bruce Leonard's statement had cleared up his ownership of the dog. That much was fine. But there was still a big question mark left dangling in the air. It took courage, but finally he managed to get the important words past his tightened throat muscles. "Are y-you g-going to keep me here?" he blurted.

There was a worried frown on the man's face. He gave Rusty a keen look. "I don't know, lad," he said slowly. "I really don't. I've been thinking of it—but there are still some questions to be settled. I wish you hadn't asked me yet. But of course you want to know.

"I'll tell you what. I'll try to get everything settled in my mind by the end of shipping—before school starts. Then we'll have a talk, and I'll tell you for sure. I might as well say now that I know all about you. Naturally I had to investigate."

He walked away, leaving Rusty feeling sick in the pit of his stomach. Now everything was in a turmoil again. A sense of desperation took hold of him. Perhaps it would be smart to take Pal and Toby and leave. With a horse and a dog like Pal he ought to be able to get a job with some other sheep outfit. Still, it was the slack season, and men, even experienced ones, were being laid off instead of hired. What chance would an undersized boy have?

Yet, if he stayed, was he not running a great risk? Bruce Leonard had said that he knew all about him. Mr. Leonard might consider it his duty to send him back to his uncle.

"I won't go. I won't." Rusty gritted his teeth and dug his fingernails into the fence rails.

Pal's whining grew louder, Rusty looked down at the worried animal. "It's all right," he said. "We aren't going with the sheep. We're staying here until after shipping. Then—maybe we'll start wandering."

A commotion in the corral behind him drew his attention. He turned. Randy was back there, breaking a horse which had just been brought in from the range. Rusty turned and threw his legs over on the other side of rail to watch the show.

Whew! Randy certainly could ride! The bronc was a mean one. He knew plenty of tricks to unseat the rider. But Randy hugged with his knees, scratched the bronc's sides with his spurs, and waved his hat. At last the horse gave up his struggles to rid himself of that unwanted weight on his back.

"Good going!" Rusty shouted. "Hey. Wh-what about letting me ride one of the broncs?"

Randy cocked his head and stared up at the boy. "Hanker to get your neck broken?" he asked.

"I w-won't get my neck broken." Rusty was excited. "I was riding w-wild horses before I c-could walk." He crossed his fingers as he said it, because of course it wasn't exactly true, although he had helped break wild horses from the time he was nine.

"P-please," he begged. "I'll stick. I promise."

"I remember you told me you tamed that old broomtail you ride," Randy said. "And he's pretty good as nags go. But these broncs are different. They really have springs in 'em."

"That's wh-what I like." Rusty was making ready to climb down from his perch.

"I'll give you a horse to ride." Randy's sharp eyes were going over the horses crowded in the corner. He picked out a bay and let his rope snake out. In a few deft motions he had the wide-nostriled creature drawn to the snubbing post and a saddle on his back.

"That l-looks like Pard," Rusty said suspiciously. "You don't need to give me a t-tame horse."

154

Randy let his rope snake out

"Climb aboard," Randy said with a grin. "And be prepared for a battle. You won't find this fellow tame."

And indeed he was not. Rusty felt as if his head were being jerked from his shoulders. He was on a bucker for sure. He gritted his teeth and hugged with his knees and used every trick he had ever learned to stay aboard. Several times he thought he was going to be sent throught the air, but each time he was able to recover his balance. Never had he had such a hard ride.

At last Randy popped a whip. It sounded like the crack of a pistol. At the sound the bronco instantly stopped bucking. Randy seized hold of the reins next to the bit, and Rusty quickly and gratefully slid to the ground.

"You're good!" Randy said in amazement. "The best kid rider I ever saw. And you waste talent like yours on sheep!"

"I like sh-sheep," Rusty panted. "Of course I'd rather be a rodeo rider—b-but I don't see much chance of that."

The bay horse crowded with its comrades in the far corner of the corral. Rusty and Randy went out through the gate.

Randy studied Rusty shrewdly as they walked slowly toward the house. "I've got a notion," he drawled. "A darned good notion . . ."

"Wh-what is it?" Rusty asked curiously.

"Just wait," Randy told him. "Let me think it over for a while."

During supper Bruce Leonard told the men that the drive to the shipping point would commence at daybreak two days later.

"Hank, you will drive the sheep wagon. Nellie will go along to cook the meals. Ginger, you can go too and make yourself handy wherever you can. You and Ben will stay overnight with Aunt Linda. Mont and Juan and Walt will herd."

Rusty's heart stood still. Where did he come in? Was he not to be given some job and allowed to go?

"Rusty—" the boss looked him squarely in the face— "you are good with horses. You ride Toby and take charge of the extra horses. We always take two or three in case we need them."

"I'll say the kid is good with horses!" Randy broke in. "He's the ridingest kid I ever saw. He has most bronc peelers I know skinned all to pieces."

"When did you see him ride a bronc?" Bruce Leonard's voice was cool.

"This afternoon," Randy said. "I was giving those new broncs a workout. He asked to ride one. So I let him."

"I thought I hired you for that work." Mr. Leonard's eyes snapped with anger. "When I want the boys to do it, I'll give orders to that effect."

Randy shrugged. "O.K.," he said with indifference. "But it's a darned shame to take a kid with Rusty's talent for riding and make a sheepherder of him."

"You forget—" there was a quiver to Mr. Leonard's voice—"that this is a sheep outfit. We happen to like sheep. We have a great deal of respect for the men who care for our flocks. And not a great deal for drifting rodeo riders."

Rusty wanted to jump to Randy's defense. After all, he was a pretty swell guy. Still, he felt toward sheep and their tenders just as the boss did. And he felt a bit of self-conscious pride that he was the storm center of the argument. It was not often that he was given this much importance.

The driving of the sheep to the shipping point started out without too much promise of excitement. It would take all day, because the sheep must not be hurried. Haste would take its toll of weight, hence market value. The main thing was to keep the animals headed in the right direction and to keep the band from splitting—a difficult task, since the drive was along a road where cars would be met now and then. Inconsiderate and impatient drivers often set up a loud honking of horns which might cause all sorts of commotion among the sheep.

Randy was through at the Ram's Horn. Rusty had heard some sharp words in Mr. Leonard's study the previous night. He knew that Randy was given his pay, but he realized that was all that he was likely to know about the matter.

"I've got a scheme cooking," Randy told Rusty as they rode along at the tail of the herd.

"T-tell me," Rusty said eagerly.

"Nope. You just wait and see. I'll spring it when the time's ripe." And that was all Randy would say.

They reached the loading pens next to the railroad by dusk. The wagon was already there, a thin wisp of smoke coming from the smokestack.

As the corral gates were being shut upon the protesting sheep, Ginger came to the wagon door. She banged on a dishpan with a mixing spoon. "Come and get it or I'll throw it out," she yelled.

The herders quickly washed hands and faces and lined up. They helped themselves from the huge pot of chile and spaghetti and hot rolls.

As Rusty was filling his plate, Ginger whispered, "I know a secret. The swellest secret. Anyway, I think it's going to happen. It's about you. But I won't tell." Her eyes sparkled.

"You're about to bust," Ben said in a disgusted tone. "You'd better hush. Why can't girls ever keep a secret?"

"I haven't told anything." She wrinkled her nose saucily.

"You'd better t-tell me, or I won't sleep," Rusty said.

But neither Ben nor Ginger would say another word.

XV

The Crowd Cheered

Early the following morning the loading of the sheep into the freight cars began. It was a dusty, noisy job. The animals resisted being pushed onto the runways leading to the cars. It was necessary to get a leader to take the notion to step through the entrance. Then the others followed.

Each car had two levels to be loaded. Then the great doors were pushed shut, and the car rolled down the siding a short distance to make way for another empty car.

By noon all the sheep were loaded. Soon an engine would be hooked onto the cars and the sheep taken to market. They had already been sold to the jobber who had in his train of cars the sheep he had bought from other ranchers.

"Poor old woollies," Rusty said sadly as the train pulled

away. "You're nice old things. I like you. Now you're going to market to be made into mutton."

"Not all of them," Bruce Leonard said. "Some of the old ewes will be sold to small ranchers who hope to get another crop or two of lambs and wool from them. And of course many of the lambs will go to other ranches to be fattened for market.

"Yeh," Rusty said. "I-I k-know that you can't k-keep all of the sheep or you'd soon go broke."

"Right," the man agreed. Then he told Rusty, "I have some business to take care of in town. And I want to see Mr. Hawken, the rancher who was hurt in an auto wreck by our place. Ginger and Ben are going to spend the afternoon with their cousins. I'm letting the men have the rest of the day off. Do you think you can make it alone back to the ranch with the horses?"

"Of c-course," Rusty said. He was proud to be given the responsibility, although he would have liked to stay to see the rodeo.

After lunch was over, Hank set out to drive the sheep wagon back to the ranch. Mr. Leonard drove off in the car with Ben and Ginger. The men who were to stay in town took the truck. Rusty was left alone with the horses, and with Pal to keep him company.

He was taking the horses to the river to water them when Randy rode up.

"Hi, pardner!" he said good-naturedly.

"Hi!" Rusty grinned his pleasure at being addressed in this way by his hero.

"Want to hear about my little scheme?"

Rusty nodded. With the halter reins in his hands he went closer to Randy.

"It's like this," the rider said confidentially. "You're a good kid. I like you a lot. I want to help you get a break."

"A br-break?" Rusty asked.

"Sure. A chance to prove that you're something above a mere sheepherder."

A frown creased Rusty's brow. What was Randy getting at?

"I've fixed it so that you'll have a chance to show what you can do at the rodeo in town this afternoon. This is just a small rodeo that we cowboys are putting on ourselves. But it's stirring up a lot of interest. Folks like to see the fellows they know compete. So there'll be a big crowd. And the prizes are worth while."

"I don't get it," Rusty said.

Randy leaned over confidentially to explain. "It's like this. Each of us pays an entry fee. That's the way it's done at all rodeos. Then the winners of the events split the amount three ways. I'll stake you for the entrance fee. You can pay me back from your winnings."

"What winnings?" Rusty asked.

"Well," Randy explained, "you know you can ride that horse you rode yesterday. It's a cinch, now that you're on to his tricks. And, let me tell you, there isn't anything in the world like getting out in front of the grandstand and putting on a good show and hearing people yell. It really makes a fellow feel important."

162

He was looking down at Rusty with a shrewd expression on his features.

Rusty drew in his breath. To be important! How often he had dreamed of doing some brave or spectacular thing which would throw the spotlight on him. To do just one thing which would give him importance. Maybe then the great empty feeling would fade away.

"I-I can't," he said dully, shoving the splendid dream away from him. "The boss told me to drive the horses back to the ranch."

"Did he say when you had to start or when you must get there?" Randy asked.

"No-o."

"Well, don't be a dope all of your life. The boss is giving the hands the afternoon off. Didn't you hear him say so at lunch?"

"Y-yes. B-but he d-didn't say me."

"He didn't say any other names, either," Randy said impatiently. "He didn't call the roll. He just said, 'Take the rest of the day off, fellows.' Aren't you one of the hands?"

"I r-reckon I am."

"Then you're entitled to the same privileges as the rest. You can enter the rodeo and still get to the ranch before dark if you take the Sandy Creek cutoff."

Still Rusty hesitated.

"Truth of the matter is—I want to ride that Appaloosa horse," Randy went on. "You'd do your pardner a little favor like that, wouldn't you?"

Rusty looked up in surprise. "I-I thought you were supposed to ride b-buckers in the r-rodeo," he said. "That A-Appaloosa is as g-gentle as Toby."

Randy grinned and turned on the full force of his personality. He leaned over with an engaging, confidential air, although no one was around to overhear. "I have the best joke you've heard in ten years," he whispered. "Any horse will buck if you put a burr under the saddle. That's why the bay bucked you yesterday. So—I'll ride the Appaloosa. You ride the bay. None of the other boys will want to ride such tame-looking animals. So we'll split first and second money."

"But I thought that the rodeo riders drew for their horses," Rusty said. He was still a trifle doubtful, although his misgivings were evaporating under Randy's spell.

"They draw at state fairs and such." Randy brushed the doubt away like a feather. "But this is a sort of private rodeo between local cowboys. We make our own rules."

"It—it doesn't seem quite on the level," Rusty said.

"Oh, shucks! Don't be such a sissy. This is just one of those stunts cowboys are always pulling on each other. You know how we are. The boys will be howling about this one when you're a granddad. And they'll be telling about how you outsmarted 'em."

Randy made it seem very attractive. And certainly there could be no serious objection. The boss had said everyone was to take the afternoon off.

"The boss won't care." Randy seemed to read his mind. "In fact, he'll be glad to have his horses given a workout. They haven't been getting enough exercise and they're a

164

bit spooky. I'll guarantee that he won't mind. I'll take all the blame. Come on. Be a good sport."

That did it. Rusty wanted to be a good sport in his hero's eyes.

"I'll d-do it," he said.

"Fine! Fine!" Randy cried. "I'll promise you that this will be a big day in your life. Bring the Appaloosa and the bay. We might even put a burr under Toby's saddle. It would give the crowd a laugh to see that old moth-eaten nag of yours buck."

Rusty was not hurt at Randy's uncomplimentary reference to Toby. He knew that the cowboy was only teasing— trying to "get a rise."

"D-don't think that Toby couldn't put on a show," he said in proper cowboy vein.

Randy borrowed a pair of cowboy boots for Rusty. It made Rusty feel important to be walking around among the cowboys and have Randy introduce him as "My pardner."

Randy pointed toward the grandstand. "See? What did I tell you. The grandstands are full. People like these affairs better than the rodeos that bring in a lot of professionals. The cowboys themselves are running this, so part of the gate receipts go into the purses of the winners. . . . Stick to the saddle as if you were glued there, and you'll have enough money to buy yourself a real horse to ride."

"I've got a r-real horse," Rusty said.

"You'll do," Randy said approvingly. "I've got a notion to take you on rodeo circuit with me. You're quite a pal."

Although there was a bank of black clouds overhead,

Rusty felt as if the sun had suddenly burst through and warmed him with its glow.

The bronc riding started. Rusty climbed onto the top rail of a fence and hooked his heels over a pole. He felt proud and important to be sitting beside his hero and to be one of the performers. He nodded agreement with every remark Randy made regarding the riders and their performances and the horses.

Then it was Randy's turn. He gave Rusty a wink as he got down from the fence. "Watch this," he said. "It's going to be good."

And it was. The Appaloosa was a powerful horse with plenty of fire and spirit. Naturally he did not like having a burr between the saddle and his flesh, and he went through a whole program of tricks to get rid of it. Randy waved his hat and scratched with his spurs and shouted, "*Yi-pee, yi-ee!*" His supple body gave with every motion of the horse, and he had everyone in the grandstand on his feet, roaring approval.

Rusty was yelling at the top of his voice. Without a doubt Randy had put on the best ride yet.

The crowd was still cheering. Rusty stared at them. Would they yell like that for him? A thrill went tingling up his spine. He must do well. He must. Not only for the thrill of hearing the crowd roar for him but to make Randy proud of him. It was swell of the cowboy to give him this chance!

Randy came swaggering over, looking very matter-of-fact, but Rusty could see that underneath he was excited with his triumph.

"You were swell!" Rusty said proudly. "Gosh, but you were swell!"

Two more rides, and it was Rusty's turn. He walked over to the chute, trying to look self-confident, but it was all that he could do to keep his legs from buckling under him. He clambered up on the fence and straddled the chute where the bay stood with drooping head, perhaps dreaming of a field of clover.

Randy was on the opposite side, getting ready to drop the saddle on the bay's back. He gave Rusty a meaning wink.

"Sit light until the chute gate is opened," he whispered. "Then bear your weight on the back of the saddle."

Rusty nodded. He understood that with every buck the horse made the rider would come down with a bump which would increase the pain caused by the burr. His teeth were chattering when he eased himself into the saddle and took the reins.

The gate swung open. Rusty bore his weight in the saddle as Randy had told him to do. The bay lowered his head between his front legs and went into action. He went through the same tactics he had used when Rusty rode him before, but with more vigor. Rusty pretty well knew what to expect. It wasn't easy to keep his seat. He felt lighter and weaker than he had felt when the horse bucked in the corral. The animal's leaps were longer. He had more room for action here, and he took advantage of every trick in the bucking horse's list. Rusty was sure that no horse had ever bucked so hard or gone through so many contortions. His spine felt cracked and his teeth loose. Would that pistol

167

never fire? Was this to go on all afternoon?

The pistol did pop, but Rusty could not hear it for the roaring of the crowd. Randy rode up alongside, seized him under the armpits, and eased him to the ground. To Rusty's surprise he found that he was still able to walk. He swayed a bit, but his legs held him upright.

Randy bent over and yelled at him. "Wave your hand to the crowd, pard. It's you they're yelling for."

In a daze, Rusty did as he was told. Were they actually yelling for him? Golly! All his life he had dreamed of a moment like this. And now it was actually happening. He could hardly believe it.

A few minutes later Randy rode up on his own horse, leading the bay. "It's in the bag, pard," he gloated. "There wasn't anything here to beat our rides. Together we'll get first and second money. And I'm going to split with you— just as I promised."

Rusty looked at the cowboy with admiring, grateful eyes.

Sure enough. When the rodeo was over Randy went to the office and came back with a whole pocketful of money. This he proceeded to divide. To Rusty's amazement, he had over sixty dollars. No wonder cowboys liked rodeo riding. It was profitable as well as thrilling. Had Randy meant it when he said that he would take him along on the rodeo circuit?

They were riding side by side through the west entrance when Bruce Leonard stepped forward. He took hold of the reins of the bay horse Randy was leading.

Randy let out a shrill whistle. "Excuse me!" he cried,

The bay lowered his head . . . and went into action

putting spurs to his horse. "I've got to see a man about a mule."

In a second he was out of sight, leaving Rusty alone to stare into Bruce Leonard's angry eyes. Behind their father stood Ben and Ginger, with sober, reproachful looks in their eyes. Suddenly what he had done did not seem so smart to Rusty. The money in his pockets felt no heavier than his heart. And the leaden clouds hanging close to the earth matched his mood.

"I had thought you were dependable!" Bruce Leonard's eyes blazed. His voice was angry. "And you had the gall to take my horses for a fool lark like this. You endanger my property, and spoil the horses I entrusted you with. All I can say is that I am a very poor judge of human nature."

"R-Randy s-said it w-would b-be all r-right." Rusty's tongue stumbled all over itself. He realized how weak the words sounded. He was only making the matter worse by putting the blame on Randy. And what of Randy? He had said that the full responsibility would be his. But at the first hint of trouble he had run away.

"Ben, you go with Rusty to see that he finishes his job. That he drives the horses back to the ranch. I'll take the matter up with him there." Mr. Leonard turned and stalked toward the car, with Ginger at his heels.

Ben climbed into the saddle on the Appaloosa. Rusty was riding Toby. He led the bay, and Ben took the bridle rope of two other extra horses they had along. Pal followed at the rear.

Nothing was said until the boys were outside of the

town. Then Ben spoke up. "Gosh, Rusty! What did you do it for?"

"I w-wish I k-knew. The way R-Randy p-put it, it sounded all r-right. A s-smart thing to do."

There he was, putting the blame on Randy again. Yet he realized now that actually it was his own fault, since he had been given the responsibility of the horses.

"It was smart all right." Ben's tone was scornful. "Smart alecky. Randy's no good. A show-off and undependable. That's why Dad fired him. I s'pose that's why he did such a stunt. To get even. Dad just about blew his top when he saw his horses out there, bucking like wild ones. How on earth did you get them to put on such a show?"

"R-Randy put burrs under the saddles," Rusty said, his voice heavy with misery.

"Sometimes it ruins horses to make 'em buck after they've been broken. And you can be sure that Randy knew that."

"Th-they act all right now," Rusty said.

"Yeh. They're tired out. But they're just apt to start bucking again any time."

Rusty's head was sunk on his chest. What was there to say? What could he do to make things right? Here in a short time he had undone all of his efforts of several months.

"Gosh!" Ben said. "If only you hadn't done such a stunt! Dad was just about to adopt you. He was fixing up things today. You would have been my brother. And now you've most likely ruined everything. Ginger and I have wanted to tell you, but Dad wouldn't let us."

Rusty drew in his horse and stared at Ben unbelievingly.

171

"He-he w-was g-going to adopt m-me?"

Ben nodded.

Rusty flapped the reins to start his horse, shaking his head hopelessly. He could not have spoken had he wished to. Anyway, what was there to say? What he had dreamed of and longed for had been his—and he had ruined it all by one foolish action.

Now and then Ben tried to start a bit of conversation, but Rusty was so wrapped up in unhappiness that he only rode on, his eyes straight ahead and his face a mask of misery.

Finally Ben kicked the ribs of the horse he was riding. "We'd better shove these horses on a bit," he said. "Looks like our early fall storm's about to hit."

Rusty obediently plied heels to Toby's sides. "I f-felt s-some snow on my f-face," he muttered, "but it w-won't amount to much."

"Don't fool yourself," Ben told him. "We always get an early fall storm. Then usually it clears off and is nice for a month or so. And sometimes these early storms can be plenty mean. I've seen some tough fall blizzards."

Rusty knew that in this area early storms were usual and that often they were severe, but right now he did not care. All that he could think about was his own trouble.

XVI

Lost in the Storm

By the time the boys got to the Ram's Horn Ranch, snow was swirling about them. They could scarcely see the ground ahead of their horses.

"Stick close to me," Ben shouted. "I'm giving my horse his head. He'll find the way home. Toby doesn't know the way so well."

Rusty did as he was told, and the bay led them straight to the barn door. The boys removed the saddles and rubbed the horses down. They watered the animals, and filled the mangers with hay. Then they made a dash for the house.

"I was worried about you," Mrs. Leonard said, relief coming over her face. "I'm glad you're back."

Rusty's frozen heart thawed a bit at her welcome. He looked toward Bruce Leonard, sitting before the open fire.

The man, refusing to meet his glance, arose and started to pull on a heavy coat and cap.

"Where are you going?" Ben asked.

"To the sheep camp. Tom and Juan are short of supplies. I brought the things from town. I've been waiting for the horses. I couldn't make it in the car in this storm."

"Oh, Bruce, I wish you wouldn't go out tonight!" his wife cried.

"If I wait until morning I might not be able to get there at all. The herders need food, and they need help. I've got to go now. I had planned to use the Appaloosa and the bay, but they will be too worn out. I'll have to use the others."

Rusty's heart shrivelled up. "I-I c-can go on Toby," he offered.

"You stay here, Rusty," Mr. Leonard said. "I haven't time to discuss matters with you now, but I want to when I get back. And, thanks, I'll use your Toby horse for a pack animal."

"Take Pal, too!" Rusty cried eagerly.

The boss looked at him keenly. "I'll do that, too," he said. "I'll need him to help with the sheep. You boys help Mrs. Leonard and Nellie." He opened the door, letting in a whirl of snow. Then he was gone.

"You boys want your supper," Nellie said, bustling around the stove.

When the food was ready, Ben heaped his plate, but not Rusty. He was not hungry, and the food was tasteless.

He noticed that Mrs. Leonard too, was not eating, and that she looked white and drawn.

Ben and Ginger and Nellie tried to draw her into their talk, but their efforts at creating a cheerful atmosphere were unsuccessful. With the wind increasing in fury by the moment, everyone's mind was on the storm.

Finally Mrs. Leonard pushed back her chair and went to the window, pulling aside the curtains. Nellie went to stand beside her.

"I declare to goodness," Nellie exclaimed, "I never did hear the wind howl so! The snow swirls from the ground as well as from the sky. You couldn't see your hand in front of your face out there."

"Do be quiet, Nellie." Mrs. Leonard spoke with unusual sharpness.

"I'm sorry," Nellie said. "I didn't think. But don't you worry. The mister will be all right. He knows how to take care of himself."

"He has Toby and Pal," Rusty reminded her.

"You sleep with Ben tonight," Mrs. Leonard told Rusty. "You'd be alone in the cold bunkhouse. And you could get lost on the way there."

As the two boys got ready for bed Ben said, "Golly! Wouldn't it be fun if we could be roommates like this all the time! I thought it was going to be that way. You'd make a swell brother."

"Let's not talk about it," Rusty said with so much misery in his voice that Ben said no more.

All night the wind howled and raged at the house as if trying to tear it apart. Ben's regular breathing told that he was asleep almost immediately. Rusty, though, lay shivering. In the dark, with the wind wailing around the eaves of the house, his worries and troubles grew greater.

Finally, however, weariness had its way with him and he dozed. Then he leaped to his feet. What was it that awakened him? There it was again—a terrific bang. He pulled on his clothes and ran into the dining room.

Mrs. Leonard was walking the floor. Evidently she had not gone to bed.

"The noise!" Rusty cried. "What was it?"

"I wish I knew," she said.

Ben came out, then Nellie. Last of all, Ginger appeared, still blinking sleepily.

Again came the bang, making itself heard above the howling wind.

"I reckon the barn door has blown open," Ben said. He put on a heavy coat and cap in a businesslike manner. "I'll go out and see to it before the animals get chilled."

Rusty wished that he had been the one to think of making himself useful. "I can get in wood," he finally said.

He lighted a lantern and went out the door which led into the woodshed. He carried in armload after armload of wood until all of the boxes were overflowing. Then there was nothing to do but wait for the slow minutes to tick past and watch Mrs. Leonard's face age before their eyes.

"Now you stop worrying." Nellie's voice was calm and comforting. "The mister couldn't possibly be back yet. You know very well that he'll stay through the storm to help with the sheep. These early storms never last long. This will probably break by noon. He'll be back by late afternoon."

Mrs. Leonard smiled wanly, though she scarcely seemed to have heard Nellie's words.

"Anything could happen," Mrs. Leonard said. "Just anything. And now Ben. In heaven's name! Why is he staying out there so long?"

Rusty had been wondering the same thing. Ben must have found the door, or whatever had been banging, for that noise had ceased. But there had been time to go to the barn and back a dozen times.

At last Rusty could stand the waiting no longer. He put on a warm coat and cap. "I'm going to find Ben," he said.

Rusty let himself out of the door. Suddenly he was in the grip of something far more powerful than himself. He was swallowed up by thick blackness. The wind tore at him with icy fingers. He had to grip his coat tightly around him to keep it from being torn off. The snow battered his face with icy pellets. Tears came to his eyes and seemed to freeze there. He leaned into the wind to keep from being swept off his feet.

He took a few steps and seemed to be walking off into nothingness. He turned and put his hand out to touch the house to get his bearings, but the house was not there. Frightened, he took several steps in the direction from which he was sure he had come. But still the house was not within his reach.

He stood still, trying to gather his wits. Surely he could not be more than a few feet from the house. He must have walked away from it instead of toward it. Had his sense of direction entirely deserted him? He did not dare try to retrace his steps for fear of getting farther away.

He cupped his hands and yelled, *"Yoo hoo!"* at the top of his lungs. But the wind seized the words and made them weak and useless. Again and again he yelled. As he shouted, he turned in a circle, hoping that the door would open, showing a cheery oblong of light. But nothing happened. He would have to figure out something else. Already he was growing numb with cold. He could not stand still very long.

Rusty was about four feet, six inches tall. If he stretched his arms above his head, he reasoned, that would add nearly two feet more. With his feet he scraped a circle in the snow and patted a little embankment about it. This would be his landmark. Then he lay on the ground, stomach down, and reached out with one hand. He thrust it as far past his head as possible in a long sweeping motion. It touched nothing.

Rusty inched himself around, taking care to keep his toes within the circle he had made. Again he reached. And again and again.

Just as it seemed to him that he must surely have completed a circle, he was rewarded. His hand touched something solid. His heart gave a leap of joy. Fearing to take his hand away from whatever it was, he hunched toward it. Then, slowly, he rose to his feet, pushing his hand upward as he did so. It was the wall of a building. It had to be the house.

Keeping his hands against it, Rusty followed the wall. In a few steps he felt the outline of the door. His icy hands fumbled for the knob. The door opened, and he staggered into the room. The womenfolk looked at him with startled eyes.

"I-I g-got lost in a few s-steps," he panted.

"Ben's out there!" Ginger screamed.

"Keep still," Nellie told her sternly.

Mrs. Leonard's face grew whiter.

"I-I'll find him," Rusty said.

"How?" Mrs. Leonard demanded. "If you got lost within a foot or two, how could you find the barn? And he may not be there. He may be lost the way you were—but farther away. Such things have happened in this country."

"We'll tie a rope around your waist and lash the other end to the doorknob," Nellie said. "Then you won't get lost. I'll get the clothesline from the shed."

"Good!" Mrs. Leonard cried. "That will do it." Then, "Warm yourself, lad," she added.

Rusty went close to the fire and pulled off his gloves. Mrs. Leonard thrust a cup of hot, black coffee into his hands. "Drink this. It will warm you," she said.

In a minute Nellie came from the shed, bringing two lengths of clothesline. She knotted these together, then she and Mrs. Leonard tied one end firmly around Rusty's waist. Ginger, in her efforts to help, managed only to get in the way. The other end of the rope, the women knotted tightly around the doorknob. They kept a length of rope inside the door to see that it did not come off the knob.

Once more Rusty let himself out into the storm. He bowed his head against the icy blast and started in the direction he thought the barn must be. But he walked

179

straight into nothingness. When he came to the end of the rope he knew that he had guessed wrong. If it had not been for the rope, he would have been lost again—this time probably hopelessly. But with the rope, he could swing around in a circle. Eventually he would have to come to the barn, or to the corrals which were beside it.

It was the corral he hit first. Then it was a matter of following the fence to the barn and letting himself in the door.

"Hi!" he called, wondering why Ben did not have a lantern lighted, because it was dark inside.

"Moo!" was the only answer he got.

"B-B-Ben!" he shouted in alarm. There was no sound except the sniffings of animals.

There was no time to lose. Ben must be out in the storm. Rusty hurried outside, keeping his back to the barn. He would follow a system. He would make a wide circle the length of the rope, feeling the ground with his feet. He found his way back to the barn and started again. The woodshed and the corrals made a sort of funnel between the barn and the house. Ben must be somewhere within that space. Every time Rusty bumped into one of those boundaries he would wrap the rope around his waist once, shortening it that much. In this manner, he would pretty well cover every foot of the way.

It seemed to Rusty that he went back and forth, back and forth, for hours, yelling constantly. At last he stumbled over something. He bent over the huddled form.

"Ben! Ben!" he cried.

The form stirred slightly and mumbled. Thank heaven he was not dead!

Rusty tried to lift Ben to his feet, but Ben had reached that pleasurable stage of freezing. He was sunk in a deep content from which he did not want to be disturbed.

Rusty slapped Ben's face, but Ben only put his arms over his face and would not fight back. Then Rusty put his hands under Ben's armpits and started to drag him. But that would not do. He was slackening the rope, without knowing where he was going. It would take too long to stop every few steps and wrap the rope around his waist. If only the women would keep the rope taut, so that he could drag Ben without stopping!

He gave the rope several strong tugs as a signal. To his

181

relief, the tugs were answered. The women were alert. Would they guess what he wanted them to do? The only thing to do was to try. He started pulling Ben. Naturally the rope slackened with each step. At first nothing happened. Then, to his relief, the rope grew taut. The women had guessed what he wanted them to do. It would be all right.

Before he reached the door, eager hands reached out to help him drag his burden into the house.

"He-he's all right," Rusty panted. "J-just darned cold. He's still conscious."

"All right," came Nellie's soothing voice. "We'll take over. Just you flop on the couch and warm yourself and we'll look after Ben."

A delicious drowsiness was creeping over Rusty. He knew that Ginger was drawing off his gloves and boots, putting a cup of warm milk into his hands, and covering him with a warm blanket. Then he sank into a delightful slumber.

XVII

Dream Come True

By nightfall the storm was over and the world lay at peace under a blanket of white.

Both boys had slept most of the day. Toward evening Rusty began to fret over the cows. Certainly Ben could not go out to do the milking.

"I made an awful b-botch of it," Rusty said to Mrs. Leonard, "the only time I milked a cow. But I can try."

"Your poor frosted hands!" she cried. "How could you milk?"

"I've been milking cows since before the rest of you were born," Nellie McAlester said briskly, as she put on a heavy coat and scarf. "Now that it's stopped snowing and there's no danger of my getting lost, I'll take over that chore. Ginger, you come and fork down the hay."

Ginger gave the boys a triumphant grin as she left the room. Plainly she did not object to being called upon to do boys' work.

Mrs. Leonard seemed glad to be bustling about getting supper. But her face was white and she wore a worried look. Rusty knew that she was thinking about her husband and wondering where he was. By morning the roads would be opened and the men back from town. If Bruce Leonard had not returned then, they would set out to look for him.

Rusty tried to shove into the back of his mind the thoughts of what the opening of the roads might mean to him. Would the authorities come after him? And what would they do with him when they had him? Return him to the hated Home? He turned his face to the wall. Once more bitter misery had him in its grip.

At bedtime the women decided that Ben should stay where he was. He was still in a half-groggy state, and it seemed best not to move him, so Rusty went to bed alone. There he lay awake for hours, wondering what was to become of him. Oh, why had he muffed the chance of becoming a member of this wonderful family?

The next day the hours of waiting ticked off with maddening slowness. By noon Mrs. Leonard was nearly hysterical with worry.

"He should be back!" she said over and over again. She paced the floor or sat in a rocker and tried to busy herself with mending, but nothing could take her mind from its imaginings.

The others tried every means of distracting her, but by

184

now the uneasiness had settled over all of them. Bruce Leonard should certainly be back. Could it be that he was lost in the blizzard?

The minutes ticked slower and slower. Ginger busied herself with making cookies, though no one seemed in a mood to enjoy them.

Time and again Mrs. Leonard walked to the windows to stare out into the blank whiteness.

Shortly before dark the men came from town in the truck. A snowplow had cleared the road. Having the men about lent new courage to those who had waited in the house through the dragging hours.

"What's the best thing to do about Bruce?" Mrs. Leonard asked anxiously.

"It's pretty late to start looking for him now," Mont told her. "We couldn't get far before dark. And the truck would most likely get stuck in a drift. After all, the boss is on horseback. He can get around better that way now than we can in the truck."

"If he can get around at all." Mrs. Leonard's husky voice held the hint of a sob.

Everyone stared at her, a bit shocked that she had put into words the thought that had been in the minds of all of them.

In an attempt to divert her mind, Mont said, "I cleared up the mystery about Pal's double, Rusty."

"You did?" Rusty cried.

"Yes," Mont went on. "Pal actually did have a double— his brother from the same litter. They came from the

Hawken Ranch, north of here. They had been put in the hands of a herder for training. He was a brutal fellow who was ruining them by wrong handling. Mr. Hawken was taking them to town to a special trainer the day his car was wrecked near the Ram's Horn gate. I met Mr. Hawken in town. He's just out of the hospital."

"I remember the wreck," Ben nodded. "Funny that we never connected the dog with it."

"Mr. Hawken told me about the dogs," Mont went on. "Pal's brother evidently went completely haywire. Took to killing sheep. Pal stayed near our gate, waiting patiently for the one man he did not fear and hate."

"W-will I have to g-give Pal back to Mr. Hawken?" Rusty asked fearfully.

Mont shook his head. "I told Mr. Hawken the whole story," he said. "About how Pal would have nothing to do with anyone until you came along and tamed him and made a fine sheep dog out of him. He said that under the circumstances the two of you belong to each other. That he wouldn't think of separating you."

Rusty's heart went back to beating normally again.

Mont's attempt to divert Mrs. Leonard's mind from her worries was in vain. She had taken up her anxious watch by the window again, and it was plain from the faraway look in her eyes that she had not heard a word that had been said.

Suddenly her slumped form straightened. "Quiet! Quiet everyone!" she cried out.

Each person sat or stood motionless, nerves taut, senses

186

Mrs. Leonard took up her anxious watch by the window

alert, listening. There was no sound save the ticking of the clock. Then Rusty heard something. A wonderful, familiar, welcome sound. But perhaps he had only imagined it. No, there it was again—the sound of a dog's barking.

"It's Pal!" he cried joyfully.

Everyone crowded to the window to peer into the dusk. A dark form was seen. No, it was more than one form. It was a man on horseback, leading two horses.

"Bruce! Bruce!" Melissa Leonard was crying now—but joyously.

Soon Bruce Leonard was inside, with everyone crowded around him.

"I thought you were lost in the storm," his wife sobbed. She clutched at her husband's shoulders and buried her face against his chest.

"I would have been if it hadn't been for Pal," he told her. "He led me to the main flock. They had scattered and drifted with the storm. He was worth about fifteen men in getting them gathered up."

Rusty sat huddled in a corner. Good old Pal! He had made good on the Ram's Horn Ranch, even if his master had not.

It was a joyful reunion, with everyone in the best of spirits now that the terrible tension had been released. The loss of sheep had been light, everything considered, Bruce Leonard said.

He turned to stare at Ben lying on the couch. "What's the matter with you?" he asked.

Mrs. Leonard told of Rusty's rescue of Ben. Rusty

squirmed and turned red and wished he were twenty miles away when everyone stared at him.

Mr. Leonard turned on him a gaze that seemed to bore into his very soul.

"You saved Ben's life," he said. "If he had been out there much longer, he would have frozen to death."

"It—it w-wasn't anything." Rusty wished the floor would swallow him and his embarrassment.

"It was a very big thing," Bruce Leonard said. "Not only because of what it meant to Ben—and me and my family. But also for what it proved about you. I was right in my first judgment of you. Come into the study. I want a bit of conversation with you."

Rusty followed Bruce Leonard into the study and sat on the edge of a chair. Mr. Leonard lighted the big lamp on his desk.

"I was pretty angry with you the other day," he began abruptly. "I felt that you'd let me down—my faith in you, I mean. When you came here, of course I knew that something was wrong—that you'd run away or had got into some sort of jam. So I took steps to find out something about you."

A determined look came over Rusty's face. "I—I w-won't go back to my uncle!" he muttered.

"Whoa there!" Mr. Leonard said. "You won't have to go back to your uncle. In fact, he's in jail right now and you are a ward of the state. Although as a rule I don't approve of a boy's running away, in your case you can't be blamed. Some boys would have become real problems."

189

"M-my uncle was t-trying to make a horse thief of me."
The words burst from Rusty's throat.

"Yes, I know," Bruce Leonard nodded.

"Th-then—it's the Home?"

The man gave him a long searching look. "The state has
placed you in my care," he said slowly, "until something
can be worked out for you. You seem to have a great desire
to be a cowboy. I can get you a job on a cattle ranch. Evidently sheep ranching isn't exciting enough for you."

Rusty squirmed in misery. "I-I was wrong to let your
horses be used at the rodeo," he said. "The herders are
swell. Worth fifty Randys. I see it now."

"I'm glad to hear you say that." Bruce Leonard nodded.
"Tom Comfort, Juan, and the others risked their lives in
this storm to save my sheep. I'm proud to be a sheepman."

"I-I would be, too," Rusty said in a low voice.

Bruce Leonard leaned forward and put his hand on
Rusty's knee. "You won't be sent back to the Home," he
said. "This will be your permanent home if you want it.
After thinking about it all summer I had finally made up
my mind to adopt you. You see, I had to make sure that
you were the right sort to be a brother to my own children.
I had to know that your character was good. I had decided
that you were the sort of boy I wanted for a son. Then that
rodeo affair made me wonder. You were easily led astray."

Rusty hung his head, gulped, and dug a toe deep into
the rug.

"But when I got to thinking it over while I was riding
home from sheep camp, I could see that I was hasty. It isn't

surprising that you made a mistake in judgment. Adults do that, too. Randy is a dashing, colorful fellow—the type who would appeal to a boy like you. I believe that you've learned your lesson. So, son, do you think you want to stay with us?"

Rusty's face was working. It was harder than ever for him to talk. "Sh-sh-sure!" he choked. "Oh, g-gosh, Mr. Leonard!"